Love Trinity On The Open Road.

A Novella.

A novella about friendship and love with a twist.

A novella about Polyamory.

by

Richard Deerton

I0566589

Chapter One

The sun shone through the window, lacing over Emily's face as she woke. Her eyes opened gently, bleary against the early morning light. She rose slowly, her hand rubbing sleepily at her face whilst she rolled her shoulders. Her back popped with a series of satisfying cracks as she twisted, her feet meeting the floor and carrying her out of bed.

She yawned as she walked out of her room, the door to the bathroom squeaking open. She let her clothes drop to the ground and stepped in the shower, the water soothing against her back, a content sigh leaving her lips. Gradually, she began to fully wake. After about fifteen minutes singing softly to herself, she stepped out, feet padding softly over the floor to her room.

Once she was dressed, opting for a simple t-shirt and jeans, she opened her laptop as she absentmindedly chewed on a piece of toast.

"What to do today Emily?" She said to herself, fingers flying across the keyboard. She smiled as she clutched her phone, watching a video of her and her two best friends singing drunkenly in the park at the top of their voices. "God, you guys..." She snorted, "What a mess we were last night".

She went downstairs, walking by her brother still passed out on the couch, snoring at the top of his lungs. The lounge was empty when she entered, and Emily walked over to the cabinets to select an old film, something light to relax her while she started her day.

While Hepburn and Peppard exchanged pleasantries on screen, Emily messaged her friends to see how hung-over they were.

Hey guys, it's Emily. You down to hang out today? Figure you could use a pick me up after how last night went.

She set down her phone and waited, her finger tapping impatiently on the arm of the couch. She leaned on her hand, counting through the minutes as they passed her by. When she felt the vibration of her phone she jumped and frantically snatched it up.

Yeah girl! Eli and I are at the skate park, come meet us!

She smiled as she tapped out her reply.

Will be there ASAP

She bent over and did her shoes up, tossing a hand through her hair and feeling the tangles come loose. Looking in the mirror she thought it still looked like a mess, but the good kind at least. She smirked at her reflection before checking her phone once more.

Come on! Get your bony ass in gear!

It's not bony! It's perfect!

Alright, you got me there. Hurry and get here so I can double check!

Her brother walked in, yawning and scratching his back, "Hi sis..."

She patted him on the back as she walked past him, pushing open the door and walking out into the sun.

"Alright, bye sis."

The park loomed in front of her, a semi-recent construct to keep the skaters contained to a single location and not carving up the roads and stairs of the city. It wasn't successful, but some people still appreciated it at least.

"Emily!" A woman in a leather jacket yelled out to her, "Hold up!"

She turned back and crouched down, bringing a camera up to her eye. A boy on a skateboard zoomed by, crouching down and shooting into the air, his board coming down onto a nearby rail. His foot slipped off the board, his balance failing and his legs coming down on either side of the railing.

He curled up on the ground, moaning softly in pain. The woman jogged over, "I got the shot! Thanks Eli!"

He weakly held his thumb in the air, "No problem Grace." He let his body flop limply back to the concrete.

Emily slowly walked over, "Is Eli alright?"

"Gimme a minute Em, not feelin' too hot right now."

Grace chuckled and slung her arm around Emily's shoulders, "So, how you feeling today? Head killing you?"

She shook her head, "No, I feel fine, how about you?"

"When I woke up I wanted to die." She pointed down at Eli, "Head felt like his balls do now."

He stood up, his hand still cupping his injury, "Thanks Gray, feels good to be used as an example."

"Oh pssh." She punched his shoulder, "You know I love you." She turned back to Emily, "So what's up? Why the burning need to hang today?"

Emily shrugged, "Just wanted to hang out with my two favorite people, catch up and stuff. That all good?"

Grace shrugged, "We're down if you are, Eli too. Where'd you wanna go?"

"The boardwalk? New hotdog place opened up there a few weeks back."

She smacked her lips, "I could go for a dog." She clicked her fingers at Eli, "Alright, pick up your board, come on." He walked over, placing his skateboard next to his feet. She shook her head, "No, pick it up. We've already established you can't ride the thing."

He grumbled as he fell in step with them, face still pinching in pain every now and then. He turned to Emily, "How was your morning? Anything good, or just more films?"

"Started watching one, seen it too many times. Wanted to see you two more."

Grace shook her head, "You've seen *all of them* too many times. When are you gonna make your own already?"

"That's what I'm going to college for Gray, then *I* can make the long boring films that no one watches."

Eli snorted, "Please, you could make a film about a snail watching paint dry and we'd still dig it."

"Aw thanks Eli!" She drew him in for a quick hug, "I'd feel that was a bit more genuine though if you weren't still cupping your junk when you said it."

He sighed, "You two are just going to rip me to shreds today aren't you?"

The three of them sat on the edge of the boardwalk, legs dangling off the sides and stray crumbs being flicked into the water. Emily sighed happily with a mouthful of chilidog, brushing a strand of hair behind her ear. She looked to her side to see Grace staring at her, "What's up Grace?"

She raised her eyebrow, "How do you *do* that?"

Emily tilted her head, "Do what?"

"Look graceful eating a fucking chili dog. It's not fair to the rest of us."

She smirked, "It's a learned skill, anyone could do it." She bumped her head against Grace's shoulder, "Even you, miss Rebel-Without-A-Cause."

Eli smirked beside them, "Funnily enough, Grace wouldn't be something she could ever possess."

Emily question surged to her side, tackling him down and pressing her hot dog into his face. He yelped and struggled beneath her, "Oh god! It was a joke! *A joke!*" She didn't let up, "You're just proving my point now!"

Emily struggled not to laugh, pulling Grace back. She looked her in the eye; they made it a grand total of three seconds before they lost themselves in laughter. Eli sat up and scowled, pieces of hot dog sliding off slowly, "I don't get how I became the slapstick character of our trio."

Grace slapped his knee, "Because you make it so easy baby!" She grinned at Emily, "I think this is a good look for him."

She nodded, "I agree, very Avant-garde. Your face looks like a surrealist's wet dream."

He lay back down slowly, "Well, at least someone's dreaming about me I suppose."

Emily lay back as well, Grace's arm still around her shoulder, "Any word yet?"

He wiped a piece of bun off his face and flicked it away, "Oh right, I didn't tell you." He shifted onto his side, "I got accepted into San Francisco State, music course is really good there."

They both looked at him, mouths agape, "You dick!" Grace pushed him over, "Why didn't you tell us?"

He shrugged, "I forgot, then we were drunk. You know, usual stuff."

Emily frowned, "And drunk you didn't think this was an important thing to tell us?"

Eli snorted, "I saw the video, drunk-me was too busy singing Toto to tell you about music school."

The two women chuckled, "That's fair."

"Besides, we already got my celebrating out of the way last night, at your celebration."

"Just because we were celebrating me getting into film school doesn't mean that we couldn't have had a... double celebration or something."

Grace sighed, "Em, if we doubled what we did last night we'd be dead."

"Fair." She stood up, the other two joining her, "I can't wait to get there though. Can't believe we're going to San Francisco!"

Eli bumped her fist, "Tell me about it, now we've just gotta wait for the rebel girl here to get in."

Grace looked down, her mood suddenly sullen, "Yeah..."

Emily squeezed her arm, "Hey what's wrong? The letters will come, don't worry..."

"It's not that. It's... Grace sighed, stepping away. The other two let her have some space, "God, I didn't want to bring this up here..."

Eli stepped forward, "Grace? Come on what's up?"

She ran her hand down her face, taking a deep breath and letting it out slowly. When she looked up her face was apologetic, "I'm not going."

The other two were silent, not sure if they understood. Emily walked over slowly, "Not going? What do you mean not going?"

"I'm not going. To college, to San Francisco, any of it."

Eli stepped up, "What? W-why not? We've been talking about it for forever!"

"I know! But I..." She leaned back against the rail, "I want to see more things. I don't want to just... trade Seattle for San

Francisco and spend the next four years of my life not doing anything." She looked into the distance "I want to go places, meet people, do shit you know? I want to do this." She sighed, "I *need* to do this."

Emily walked over next to her, putting her hand on her shoulder. Grace nuzzled into it, "I'm going to miss you. We're both going to miss you." She squeezed, "But if you really need to do this, I understand. I just want you to be happy."

Eli joined her, "Same here. It's gonna suck big time without you around, but we'll be fine." He shoved her lightly, "Long as you keep in contact. I'll find you and drag your ass back myself if you try and drop off the grid."

She laughed, "You could try!" She smiled softly, "But I promise, every day something will come through." She took both their hands, "We've had each other's backs since we were kids, I'm not forgetting that. Just need to make my own way, that's all."

"We get it, don't worry." Emily smiled, "Besides, it's not like we'll never see each other. We'll have holidays too, maybe we could join you sometime!"

"I think I'd like that." She pushed off the rail, "Ok, things got a little heavy there, how about we go do something fun?"

Eli raised an eyebrow, "Fun?"

"I can't believe this is your idea of fun..."

Emily shrugged on the other side of the pool, "It's swimming! You got something against water now?"

Eli gestured around him, "We just graduated from here! Why are we breaking back into the school to swim?"

"I like this pool! All the public ones have piss in them, and you can't tell me that's not true!"

Grace stepped up beside him, "She does have a point you know, the ratio has to be like... 2/5 piss."

He squeezed the bridge of his nose, "Alright, I'm gonna ignore the real James Joyce-esque turn this conversation took and just jump in the pool, cool? Cool."

He ran forward, leaping into the air and tucking his legs in, wrapping his arms around and hitting the water with a tremendous splash. His head shot up a second later, "Fuck this is cold!"

Grace doubled over with laughter, "No shit idiot! It's winter and the school's closed, of course there's no heating!"

So focused on her laughter, she failed to notice Emily sneaking up behind her, her two hands touching the small of her back making her freeze up. Emily leaned in close to her ear, "Would you look at that? Easy prey..."

She shoved forward, Grace tumbling over the edge and into the water below. She broke the surface and started flailing around, "Oh my fucking god it's freezing!"

Eli pointed and laughed, his teeth still chattering, "Oh! Not so funny now is it huh?"

"F-f-f-fuck you!" She turned around, "Y-y-you coming in, t-traitor?"

Emily hummed as she went behind the pool dividers, switching the heating for the pool on and cocking her head, "I think I'll wait for it to heat up a bit, actually."

Eli stared at Grace, pure annoyance on his face, "No heating huh?"

She rolled her eyes, "Oh like you can talk about mistakes, you cupped your junk in pain for three hours today!"

Gradually, the water began to heat, Grace and Eli sighing in contentment and floating on their backs. Emily looked on, a small smile on her face, before slipping in. She didn't make a big entrance like the others, so when she floated up between the two they were startled.

"What the fu- Oh, It's you Em."

She chuckled, "'Course it's me Eli, who else would it be?"

"I dunno, could've been the swimming coach. Now that we're not students they might've decided to get a little touchy feely."

Grace groaned in disgust, "Oh gross, they're like ninety years old!"

He smirked, "Just think about all the experience they'd have..."

"Stop."

"And being a swim coach for that long? You just *know* they'd be able to go for *hours*..."

She shrieked and covered her ears, "God, stop! I'm going to come over there and drown you if you keep this up!"

Emily chuckled, "I'm with her Eli, I don't need to think about the Coach's gyrating pasty ass thank you very much."

He shrugged and smiled to himself, "Alright, fine, I'll go appreciate the elderly somewhere else then."

She lay back down and smiled, Grace floating on her right and Eli on her left.

I can't believe that this is going to end soon...

She frowned, brow furrowing as she thought.

There has to be something we can do... Not to change her mind, but maybe just... Give her some more memories. A start to her journey that we can be a part of.

Her eyes snapped open as it came to her, a grin on her face.

Grace raised her eyebrow, "Em? What are you so zany about all of a sudden?"

"Oh nothing! Nothing just... Just thinking..."

I need to make some plans. This needs to be perfect.

She smiled, speaking softly to herself, "For all of us."

Chapter Two

Emily had spent hours on the Internet the night before trying to find *something* to do with her friends. So many in fact, that it was mid-morning, and she showed no signs of stopping.

She rubbed at her temples; "It needs to be something big, something wild. It needs to say that I'm going to miss you."

She smiled, "It needs to say, 'I love you, please be safe.'"

Emily growled, "So why is this so *hard?*"

She scrolled through page after page, seeing bands, films, festivals... None of them ever seemed to be right, none of them were special enough. All of these things they'd done before, what could they do that was different?

And then she found it. Just as she was about to give up hope it stuck itself out, she clicked on it.

"Meteor shower predicted over the skies of Arizona..." Her face lit up as she read the date, "That's just over a week from now!" She hoped as she checked the attached map, and her prayers were answered, "That's almost right over the Grand Canyon. The *Grand Canyon!*"

She jumped out of her chair, spinning in celebration, "It's perfect! It's so wonderfully, absolutely perfect!" She froze, "*Shit!* I've got no way to get out there!"

"Maybe no way to get out there..." She turned, her brother smirking at her, "But you could always *ask* you know?" He dangled his car keys from his fingers, she looked up at him, eyes wide.

"You... You'd let me take the car? You'd let me take The Captain?"

He laughed, "Alright, I'm going to be real for a minute. The Captain is a piece of shit, it always has been, it just looks cool. Second..." He smiled, "I know how much Grace means to you, and if this is going to be your last chance to show that then you bet your ass you can borrow the car. Just don't crash the thing, it's a piece of crap but I still need it."

She ran forward and seized him in a hug, her arms crushing around his ribs, "Oh my god, thank you, *thank you*! I don't know how to pay you back!"

He chuckled, patting her head slowly, "Tell Grace to take some photos during the trip, girl's got some serious skills. That's my price. Fair?"

Emily beamed, "Fair." She threw her thumb back, "Do you wanna help plan or..."

"Nah..." He shook his head, "That seems like a you and Eli thing. You guys know better than anyone what you want." He paused at the door, "Just come get me when you're done."

Three hours. Three hours went by and she finally had it. More or less, Emily had a complete plan for the trip, a route was picked, the cheapest motels that also didn't look like the sets of horror films looked into. She'd even had the time to come up with a budget, though therein lay the problem.

This trip was going to cost *a lot* of money.

Even when she shuffled things around, picked shorter routes, budgeted for less food, even when she eliminated the motels altogether and planned to sleep in the car, it was still too much. Her savings would only cover two or three days max.

She was sure she could get Eli in on the budget, that would probably bring them up to be able to sustain themselves for another two days. But that still left them with no less than four days that they'd be flying high and dry, and she knew that the middle of Arizona was not where you suddenly wanted to find yourself with no money.

Emily groaned, "Everything was going so well!" She wiped a hand over her face, "I can't ask Grace to pitch in for this, the trip's meant to be for her..."

She walked down into the lounge, flopping onto the couch next to her brother. He looked at her, surprised, "What's eating you? A few hours ago you were over the freaking moon."

She shrugged, "Cash problem, even if I get Eli in we'll only have enough for five-ish days. I dunno how to fix that."

"You can't get Grace in on it?"

She sighed, "I can't make her pay for her own going away present, can I?" She shook her head, "Even if she wanted to, I don't know if she has any money saved up, all her money gets sunk into her camera."

Neither of them spoke for a few minutes, the sound of the television the only thing breaking the silence. Finally, after a lot of deliberation, he sighed, "I'll help out."

Emily snapped her eyes to him, a refusal already on her lips, "No! You're already giving us the car, any more would be..."

"The car is a gift, the money you can pay back later." he smirked, "I do want the money back, but I don't need it right now. And I can already tell how set you are on this trip."

"I... Are you *sure*?"

"I wouldn't offer if I wasn't. I can spare about $200, that should get you gas for two days." He shrugged, "That's the best I can do."

She shook her head, "It's already so much more than you had to. Thank you. I mean it."

He waved her off, "Please, I know how important Grace is to you, you've been girlfriends for what? Three years now?"

That certainly wasn't what she was expecting. "Wha... I'm sorry, *girlfriends*?"

He rolled his eyes, "Oh come on, don't try and hide it. It's so obvious!"

"But... But we're not girlfriends!"

He laughed, "You cannot be serious!" He looked at her face, his eyebrow raising in confusion, "Holy shit are you being serious?"

She threw her hands up, "Of course I am! Why would you think that?" She narrowed her eyes, "How long have you thought that?"

"Like, three years! I thought you two were together, like, you're always so close..."

"We're best friends Jay! Of course we're close!"

"No not like..." He groaned, "You know what? You're right, that was my fuck up. I thought you two were together and... I'm sorry, I didn't want to upset you."

She chuckled, "It's alright, don't worry about it."

"But really you're not? 'Cause it'd be pretty cute..."

"Jay shut the fuck up."

Eli, as she predicted, was more than happy to help. A going away present was exactly what he thought Grace deserved, and Emily's idea was perfect for it.

"I can't believe that you found the most perfect place to go to as well."

She shrugged, "Anyone could have done it, it was just on the Internet."

Eli rolled his eyes, "Dude, I know that but... A meteor shower happening before we all leave? Just in time for one last big hurrah?" He laughed, "Seriously, what are the chances of that?"

She considered, before nodding, "Probably pretty low, yeah. Looks like luck's on our side today!"

They sat down, "Ok, let me in on the details, how are we doing this?"

Emily cleared her throat, "With the money from you, me and my brother, we have enough to cover about six days, seven if we stretch it thin. I think we should only stay in motels if they're cheap, otherwise we sleep in the car or a tent."

"Not the first time I've slept in a car, no problems there."

"Food should only be cheap stuff, maybe something every now and then for a special occasion. We need money for gas though, so we can't go wild."

He rubbed his chin, "What about the days we haven't got covered?"

She sighed, "I'm still thinking that over. Maybe Grace could sell some photos or something. Worst comes to worst we can always hustle pool."

He snorted, "You mean *you* can hustle pool, you're the only one out of us who's actually any good."

"True, very true." She smiled, "I've got a good feeling about this!"

"You kidding me? I've got a *great* feeling about this!" Eli jumped up, "We should go get her now!"

"Wait... *Now* now?" Her eyebrows rose to her hairline, "You really think we should do it now?"

He grabbed her hands, "Fuck yes dude! Be spontaneous, live in the moment, Carpe Diem and all that shit!"

She threw her head back and laughed, "You know what? Yeah, yeah let's do it!" She jumped up, squeezing his hands in hers, "Let's go over there right now!"

This was it, the first step in their journey. In less than five hours they would hopefully be on their way out of town, the Grand Canyon in front of them and Seattle shrinking into the distance behind them. Of course, that all depended on whether Grace actually wanted to go or not, but given their track record, she'd follow them anywhere. It had gotten them into trouble before, but hopefully this time it would bring them nothing but luck. They would certainly need it.

"Grace? Grace are you there?" Eli tapped on her door, neither of them hearing the sound of movement within the house. "Grace open up!"

He looked back at Emily, "I don't think anyone's home."

She shook her head, "She's home. It's a day off, you know how much she loves to sleep."

"Fair point, but how are we going to get in?"

She looked around the side of the house, her eyes flicking to her bedroom window on the second floor, "I need you to give me a boost..."

"*This* is your plan?" Eli spoke shakily, trying to keep his balance as she tried to climb the wall, her weight very awkwardly held in his hands, "Climb up and hope that the window's open?"

She scoffed, "Oh come on Eli, who locks their second story windows?"

"People who don't want to get robbed!" He locked eyes with the paperboy walking past, a confused look on his face, "Hey what's up little man?"

"Look just... Trust... me..." She reached up slowly, her fingers gradually finding purchase on the edge of the windowsill, "Alright, I think I've got it, push me up!"

Eli grunted and pushed with all his strength, her chest rising above the edge of the sill. The window slid open easily, her body leaning in gradually... then much too fast.

"Too much Eli! *Too much...*" She fell through with a thump, her body landing on something hard.

Something hard and moving.

"Oh my god what the *fuck*!" She found a knee pressed into her back, then found herself staring up at the ceiling from the floor. Grace looked down at her, obviously having just woken up, and obviously not happy, "Emily? What are you doing?"

She waved slowly, "Hey Gracie, me and Eli wanted to talk to you."

"Eli?" She looked around the room, "Where is he?"

A muffled voice came through the window, "I'm so sorry!"

Emily chuckled, "He's still out there."

She sighed, "Well clearly I'm not going to get anymore sleep." She stared at Emily grumpily, "This better be worth it."

"Oh, I think it is."

"A road trip?" She was looking at them with her eyebrow firmly quirked, a disbelieving smile on her face, "You two want to drop everything, getting ready for University, getting a place to live sorted out... You want to bail on all that so we can go hang out at the Grand Canyon?"

Emily frowned, "Well when you say it like that it makes us sound stupid..."

"You *are* stupid." She scratched her head, "Guys, we don't have to do that. We can just go see a movie or something, get drunk and break stuff on the beach, I don't know. This is..." She shrugged, "This is a lot you know?"

They sat on either side of her, Eli throwing an arm behind her, "Come on Gray! Think of how epic this'll be! You me and Emily, charging across the desert, no one to stop us! We can do whatever we want!"

Emily cleared her throat, "There are still laws Eli..."

"There are no rules in the desert! Who's gonna be watching? Armadillos?"

Grace laughed, "Are you guys sure about this? I mean, really sure." She dragged them of both in, "'Cause I love you both, and I'm super down for this if you really want to, but don't just do this because you think I'd like it..."

Emily grinned, "Are you insane? Of course we're doing this because we think you'd like it!" Eli joined in, "We like doing things that you like, that's what makes us happy. That's how it's always been with the three of us, hasn't it?"

"I guess..." Grace grinned, "Oh fuck it, of course I'm going to do it." She jumped up, "Let's do it! Let's go into the desert and do dumb shit!"

Emily leapt into her arms, "I'm so happy to hear that!" She leaned back, "Don't forget your camera, Jay wants pictures as payment."

"I..." Grace raised an eyebrow, "Pictures of what?"

Emily slapped her arm, "Of the *trip* you weirdo! God!"

"We'll give you an hour or so to get ready, we'll be back in a bit." Eli led Emily out of the room, "Yes I know Em, thinking of your brother doing that is super weird, I agree..."

An hour later Grace was ready and raring to go. After a quick call to her brother to get the car brought over, and Eli dropping into his home along the way, they were well into the process of getting their bags packed into the car. She couldn't stop bouncing as they loaded their bags, the time until they left counting down with each one.

"Thanks so much for letting us borrow your car!" She screamed across the yard at Jay, who responded with a weak wave.

He turned to Emily, who was busy staring at her two friends, "A sudden getaway in the middle of the afternoon huh?" He clicked his tongue, "This is all *very* romantic..."

She glared at him, "I swear to god Jay, I will break your car and you."

"Alright, alright..." He raised his hands in surrender, a smirk still on his face, "I'm not saying this to make fun of you or anything, but you know that I'm not the only one who thought that right?"

"What do you mean?"

"Seriously? You three have been joined at the hip since you were like, ten. People tend to drift apart a little and you guys... didn't." She screwed her eyes up, "We went out with *other* people!"

He shrugged, "You guys broke up, then got back together." She scoffed, he chuckled, "Look, I'm not saying it's a *perfect* theory, but I dunno, I look at you three and I see *something.*" He tilted his head at her, "Is that too weird?"

"It's annoying, and kind of creepy but... I can see where they could get confused. But there's nothing like that going on!" She looked across the yard at her two friends, Grace with a dazzling smile on her face, tears in her eyes and hands clutched around her stomach as she laughed. Eli with his goofy, easy charm, an equally wide grin on his face, which was rather difficult to see considering he was standing on his head on top of the car.

She looked at them and felt... warm. As soon as she felt it she pushed the feelings down. She shook her head.

"No, there's nothing going on."

Chapter Three

"Thanks for letting us borrow your car!"

Jay shook his head, "Don't worry about it, Grace, you just have fun alright?" He patted Emily on the back, "I'm *sure* she won't let you do otherwise."

"Please, Grace can have a terrible time if she wants, that's up to her" said Emily.

Eli called from the car, "Can you nerds hurry up already? We gotta get on the road!"

"Alright, we're coming!" Emily turned to her brother, "Thank you so much Jay, we'll take care of the car."

He watched Grace walk off to the car, slipping into the backseat and playing with Eli's hair, "Hell with the car, take care of *them*. I know how much they mean to you." He fixed her with a stern look, "And it's obvious how much *you* mean to *them*. So take care of yourself."

She blinked, "I'm so used to you just being passed out on the couch. It's weird when you get all brotherly."

He laughed, "Don't get used to it, I'm gonna be on that couch the whole time you're away. Just promise me alright?"

"I promise." She nodded, "Nothing's gonna happen to us."

"I'm holding you to that..." He drew her in for a quick hug, squeezing lightly around her shoulders. He pulled back after a few seconds, smiling. "Alright, get going. They look like they're getting restless."

Emily looked over to where her friends were seated in the car, Grace having gotten Eli into a headlock. She chuckled, "Guess I should leave then." She walked off, turning back to smile, "Love you bro."

Jay smiled, "Love you too sis."

Grace shrieked as they pulled out, "Oh my god I can't believe we're doing this!"

Emily looked at Jay's rapidly disappearing form, still waving in the background. She smiled at Grace's excitement, "Well, we should've done something like this a long time ago. It's weird that we never did."

Eli nodded, "Totally, and since you're..." His smile faltered for a second, "Well... yeah." He shook his head, "What better time than now right?"

"Yeah..." Grace draped her arms over the front seats, squeezing both of their shoulders, "I'm glad you guys took the plunge. I never would have thought of this!" She leaned back and giggled, "You believe that? Self-styled rebel and I haven't even taken a road trip before!"

The two in the front laughed, "No, you were too busy tearing Seattle apart to subject the rest of the country to it." Eli smirked at her outrage.

"Dick! You were right there next to me the whole time!" She kicked the back of his seat, she looked over and saw Emily struggling not to laugh, "Oh don't you start...so were you!"

"I'm not laughing *at* you, I'm laughing *with* you!" She broke when she saw Grace's raised eyebrow, "Ok I'm laughing at you, but it's coming from a place of love!"

"Yeah sure." She rolled her eyes before smiling. "I guess I can forgive you, since you're taking me to the Grand Fucking Canyon of all places! It's so cool that we're doing this! Aren't you hyped?"

Eli laughed, "Yeah Grace, we're hyped! But we literally just started driving, if we keep it at one hundred we're gonna be burned out before we leave Washington."

She slumped back in her seat, "I hate how you're making total sense."

"Well that doesn't change the fact that I *am* making total sense." He shrugged, "Now might be a good time to get a bit of sleep, we're gonna be driving for a while."

"No way! I can't sleep now, this is like... the most important part of the whole trip!"

Emily raised her eyebrow, "What about... you know, when you reach where you were heading to in the first place?"

"Oh pssh." She waved her hand lazily, "Everyone knows first impressions are important! If I can't be so hyped up that I can't sleep when my two best friends kidnap me and throw me into a surprise road trip, how am I going to be hyped during the rest of it?"

"That's... a good point." Eli quirked an eyebrow, "But what if you wear yourself out?"

Grace shrugged, "Then I'll fall asleep when I run out of hype. Until then," She put her hands behind her head and reclined across the seat with a groan, "Don't kill my buzz."

"...This wasn't a kidnapping..." Emily trailed off, "Was it?"

Eli shrugged, "I mean, an argument could be made for possible coercion, but I don't think it'd hold up in a court of law."

"Most willing kidnapping I've ever been a part of..." Grace mumbled with her eyes closed, Emily laughed.

"You know, you say that so dryly, I almost believe that wasn't a joke."

"Joke?"

They pulled up to a convenience store, all three eager to leave Seattle, but none of them stupid enough to do so without supplies.

"Alright, so what do we need?"

Emily dug the list out of her back pocket, "My list just says beans and water."

"No problems there." Grace slung her arms around her shoulders, "You think of anything else we need though Eli?"

"I mean… this is all stuff for an emergency so… Not really no." He started to walk in, "We can always drop into another store if we think of something else."

"What about camping stuff?"

Emily grinned, "Jay already loaded us up. We've got a tent and some sleeping bags. Tent'll be a tight fit though."

Grace waved her hand, "No big deal, we've been tripling up since we were kids, who cares?"

"True."

They browsed through the aisles, sweeping from side to side in an effort to not miss anything.

"Hey, what about some canned fruit?"

Grace nodded, "I don't want to get scurvy on this trip, toss it in the basket. Did you guys grab matches?"

Eli shook his head, "No, but I've got my lighter."

"Eh," Emily grabbed the matches, "In the basket anyway."

After what turned out to be a half hour of shopping, during which they discovered just how little they thought about common necessities, they walked out of the convenience store $50 poorer and much more prepared.

"Didn't think that we'd need toilet paper honestly."

"Well…" Emily inclined her head, "I can say with certainty that I'd rather have it and not need it, than need it and not have it."

24

"Oh, gross, yeah." Grace tossed her bags into the trunk, "So…
where to now?"

"I figure we get out of Washington first, then pull over and
finalize everything."

"10-4 good buddy." Grace threw herself into the backseat
again.

Emily chuckled and looked at Eli, "This was such a good idea,
if I do say so myself."

He grinned, "Damn straight it was, the best way to cap
everything off. Just hope everything works out."

She clapped him on the back, "It'll all work out, you just wait
and see! I've got a good feeling about this!"

Eli snorted and opened his door, "Famous last words."

"Uh hey guys? We're about to go through Tacoma." Eli turned
to look at the two in the backseat, Emily having migrated over
time.

"You think we should stop in?" Emily stretched, "Grab
something to eat?"

"Shit," Grace lifted her head off Emily's lap, "I could eat. You
guys *did* make me leave before I could get breakfast."

"Made you…" Eli looked almost offended; "We gave you like
an hour to get ready!"

"Ok, ok…" She rolled her eyes, "Maybe it's a little bit my fault
as well."

"Yeah, whatever. We'll stop here anyway. I want a muffin."

They pulled up at a quiet café on the edge of town, not wanting
to get too deep in. They had a minor schedule to keep to, and
though they didn't necessarily have to leave Washington that
night, they didn't exactly want to spend it in Tacoma.

"Alright," Emily groaned as she took a seat in the booth, stretching her legs out in front of her, "Guess now's as good a time as any to figure out where we want to go right?"

"In a second…" Eli turned to their waitress, "Uhh yeah can I get a blueberry muffin?" He turned to the others, "What do you guys want?"

Grace shrugged, "I'll have a slice of apple pie."

"Same here."

"Coming right up." Their waitress flipped her notebook closed and walked off, leaving the three alone.

Emily reached into her bag and pulled out the map she'd brought along, placing it onto the table. She pointed, "Alright, so we're here in Tacoma." She drew her finger down the map slightly, "Now we're not far from the border, but personally I think we should stay the night in Vancouver. It's getting on in the evening now."

Grace nodded, "Yeah I mean, I love you guys and all, but I'd rather spend the night in a motel rather than cramped in a tent outside."

"No problems with this plan," Eli nodded, "Once we get past the border tomorrow though, any ideas where we should go from there?"

"Once we get through Vancouver there's roads that lead all over, we could either head down through Portland or east along to Idaho, make the rest of the way down that way?"

Grace snorted, "Not sure how much you've planned, but I'd rather drive the car off a cliff than go through Idaho."

Emily smiled, "Duly noted. Where do you want to go?"

"Well I mean, you guys are the ones driving and everything."

Eli waved it away, "This trip is mostly for you Gray, you get final say on where we go."

She blushed, "Um, alright then..." She leaned over the map, studying each city east and west that they could pass through on the way to the Grand Canyon. She was so absorbed in planning that she didn't even notice when their waitress came back and handed them their food, a warm smile on her face. After a few minutes, during which her friends' food disappeared, she finally sat up, a triumphant grin on her face. "Alright, how about this?" She started tracing her finger down the west coast, "We go down through Portland tomorrow, spend a night or two there first, then head on down to San Francisco. Then we head on over to Vegas, try and get some more money, then park up at the Grand Canyon in time for the big show?" She scratched the back of her neck nervously, "I mean, if that's alright with you guys."

Emily nodded eagerly, "Yeah! That was one of the routes I was thinking of more or less." She turned, "What about you Eli?"

He smiled, "No problems here, we should have enough money for gas, and the Vegas plan isn't a bad idea." He thumped the table in excitement, "Yeah! Let's do it!"

Grace stood up, "Right now! Let's go right now!"

"No, no not yet." Emily pulled her back down into her seat, "Eat your pie, it's really good. Like, tip over 20% good."

"Fiiiine, but then we've gotta..." She took a bite of the pie and immediately went silent, "Oh holy *crap* that is good. Let's get some more slices to go."

After getting more slices of pie and leaving a very generous tip for their waitress, they got back on the road. Vancouver wasn't too far away, but night was falling, and they wanted to secure a place in a motel before it was too late.

"So like, is there anything in Vancouver worth seeing while we're here?"

Eli inclined his head in thought, "I'm... not sure actually, I don't know much about Vancouver. I'm sure there's something."

"I'll do a little looking into it tomorrow," Emily shrugged, "We might be able to check out some stuff before we swing into Portland, not like that trip'll take all day anyway."

"True, tomorrow should be a pretty easy day." Grace reached up and poked Emily's nose, "Maybe I can catch up on that sleep you made me miss out on." she cut off any apologies they were about to make, "Now now, I'm super happy that we're doing this and I wouldn't trade it for anything. But if you think I'm not going to enjoy my sleep on this trip you are so very wrong."

"Well I think you'll be able to enjoy it soon, I just found where we're staying." Eli pulled into the parking lot of a reasonable looking motel, not five stars by any means, but it didn't look like they were going to be murdered at least.

"Ok guys, I've got a plan here to save money." Emily leaned over between the two front seats, "I'll go in and get a single room, then after like 20 minutes you come to the door and I let you in."

Eli raised an eyebrow, "Are you sure? You don't think it'd be easier to just... get a room for three?"

Grace cut in, "I'm for it, we need to save money, right? After buying that pie I think this is a good place to start."

"So it's settled. I'll see you guys in a bit!" Emily left the car before anyone else could get a word in.

Grace and Eli stared at each other, "You wanna play cards?"

Securing the room was a breeze, the attendant not even looking up at her as she handed over the money for the room. Thinking back, she wouldn't be surprised if they just didn't care about what she was doing.

She stepped through the threshold of the room and looked around. It was clean at least, nothing much to look at, but it was cheap, it was indoors, and it had a bed.

One double bed. That three people would have to sleep in. Whoops.

She went and sat down, waiting for her friends to come to the door. It wasn't even 10 minutes later when she heard Grace's telltale rapid knocking, and with a new sense of excitement she ran and opened the door. They shuffled in quietly, their eyes going immediately to the bed.

"Oh right." Eli started, "We probably should have thought of that."

"I mean, we were going to be fine sleeping together in a tent."

Grace nodded, "Yeah, but we'd be in our own sleeping bags then. Not, you know, wrapped around each other under the same covers."

They stood silent for a few seconds before Emily broke the tension, "Well whatever, we're here now. We're all tired, so we may as well get this over with huh?" She pulled off her shirt and jeans and crawled underneath the covers, groaning at the warmth of the sheets, "Oh my god, so worth it."

The others followed suit, still skittish about being in their underwear, but not enough to be the only one losing out on comfort that night. They got under the covers on either side of Emily, and after a few awkward minutes of trying to stay separate they found their arms wound around each other.

It was one of the best night's sleep they'd ever had.

Chapter Four

Emily was the first to wake up, which of course meant that she couldn't move until the others woke up. Instead, for the twenty minutes that followed her opening her eyes, she lay in between her two best friends, their arms wrapped securely around her. Grace's breath tickled the back of her neck, the arm around her hip squeezing tightly as she dreamed. She could feel Eli's heartbeat underneath her cheek, a steady thump that let her know that this was in fact real, and not a dream.

Eventually the others began to stir, Grace withdrawing her arm as soon as she became aware of it. She pulled over to the other side of the bed, awkwardly stretching out as she swung her legs over the side. Eli didn't have the chance to pretend, the fact that he and Emily were facing each other made him swallow and his face heat up. He stammered out an awkward apology, pulling back and laying as far away as he could.

As awkward as it felt, Emily couldn't help but find herself missing the contact, the pleasant weight and heat reassuring her. Looking at her friends and herself, they were certainly more rested than they had been in a while. She cleared her throat, "Well, this is nice but we should probably get going. We don't wanna get caught after all."

"Y-Yeah, that sounds good." Grace glanced back at them with a slightly nervous smile, "Breakfast?"

They found a little diner not too far from where the motel was, this time opting to order scrambled eggs and sausage. The atmosphere was still awkward from waking up, and sooner or later they would have to address it. That could wait until after breakfast though, even the awkwardness of waking up clutched in your best friend's arms in your underwear can stop your stomach only for so long.

"So," Grace started through a mouthful of sausage, "Where are we going to go today?" She pointed in what she could only imagine was south, "Portland's only like fifteen minutes away, no point in going there right away is there?"

Emily shook her head, "I did a bit of reading when we were driving over, Stanley Park looks pretty cool, we could check that out for a few hours before we drive off again if you want."

"I'm down," She turned to Eli, "What do you think man? This trip isn't just about me, no matter what you two say."

He smiled, "Park sounds cool, I'm down too." He chuckled, "God, we really are a bunch of tourists, aren't we?"

Emily sniggered, "No shit Eli, that's the whole point of a road trip."

"I thought it was about rebellion, self-discovery, getting into trouble... you know, film stuff."

"That's just something that people say so that they don't have to admit that they're usually a bunch of tourists who come in and fuck everything up." She shrugged, "I'm not complaining though, I like fucking things up."

"Same here." Grace held her fist out for bumping, Emily obliged, "About time we did it somewhere other than Seattle."

"What about when we reach Portland?" Eli inclined his head, "How long should we stay there?"

31

"If it's alright with you guys I'd like to stay tonight and tomorrow. Portland's been on the to do list for a while, I think we should make the most of being there."

"Done." Emily smiled, "Look at how productive we are, if only we treated school like we're treating this trip."

Grace chuckled, "Please, like school was half as fun as this! I don't think crossing states and sleeping together was ever on the curriculum." They all froze at the last part of the sentence, "Not sleeping together like, *sleeping* together! I mean..." She held her head in her hands, "Oh *balls*."

Eli coughed nervously, "Yeah... We should probably talk about that huh?"

"Well... I thought it was nice." Emily covered her face as the others looked at her, "Yeah it's awkward now and everything but... It was a nice feeling you know? It felt... safe."

Grace nodded, "I can't deny that... it was warm at least."

"And it's not really that much different from what we've already done..." He chuckled, "Be a lot more eyebrow raising if anyone saw but... It was alright."

"Would you..." Emily trailed off, "W-would you want to... do it again?" Their eyes widened, she waved her hands, "It'd be a good way to save money and everything!" And it... you know, felt good."

Grace looked to Eli, blushing deeply, "I'm... fine with it if you are?"

He took a second to think it over, then nodded, "I guess we could give it a shot. We can always stop if it gets too weird."

Emily stood, still blushing, "Alright, we need to leave before I explode. Shall we head to the park now?"

They smiled, "That sounds great."

Stanley Park was a sight to see, the trees a wonderful color and the waters calmly making waves in the low wind. Grace was in

32

her element, taking shots left and right as they passed from water to woodland, landscapes and group selfies being taken in equal measure.

"Vancouver's pretty cool, isn't it?" Grace jumped up onto a table to get the high angle, "We should come back here some time."

They nodded, "That's not a bad idea," Emily said, "A couple days spent here would probably be alright."

Eli shrugged, "Next time I guess."

Grace jumped back down, "Hey should we get going? Portland's close but we've already been here a few hours, gotta be getting on in the day by now."

"We can head over now, I kinda wanted to go look through the forests before we go into actual Portland." Emily smiled at the thought, "You always see pictures of Oregon and it looks like one gigantic forest, I wanna see if the reality lives up to the pictures."

"Alright, let's get going then." Eli looked around them, "We really do need to come back here some time. This is beautiful."

Grace grabbed him in a headlock, "Don't worry your pretty little head about it El. We'll be back here in no time."

"Ok how about this one, every year there is an annual naked bike ride. It's been named a tradition so it doesn't have to worry about public decency laws."

Grace threw her head back and laughed, "No fucking way! When is it?"

"It's in June Gray," Emily shrugged, "Sorry but we won't be seeing the naked people any time soon."

"Oh man, that sucks." She crossed her arms, "Would've been awesome to see the naked people."

Emily laughed, "Oh check this out, roller blades are banned in public restrooms."

"I don't... *what*?" Eli raised an eyebrow, "There's gotta be a story there right? They didn't just wake up one day and decide to make that a law out of nowhere."

"Maybe it's connected to the fact that Portland has more strip clubs than any other city in America, Grace I know you'll be happy about that."

She lunged over the seat to hug them close, "Oh can we go? Can we go? Please?"

They chuckled, "If you behave then sure, we'll go see a stripper for you."

She leaned back in her seat, "Yessssss."

Eli whooped with joy as they passed the city limits, the skyline of Portland visible in the distance, "Welcome to Portland ladies!"

"Do you see anywhere good to stop? A national park or something?" Emily looked at their surroundings, "I don't wanna just leave the car on the side of the road."

After a few minutes of driving they finally saw directions to a nature reserve, it required skirting around the city of Portland at first, but that was their plan anyway.

"Here seems good, our stuff won't get stolen and there should be some good stuff to see in here."

Emily nodded, "Let's do it." She turned to Grace, "Ready to go again?"

"Pfft, you know I'm always ready."

She grinned, "That's what I like to hear."

"Ok..." Eli huffed, "Maybe I overestimated my capacity for exercise."

Grace clapped him on the back, "What are you talking about? You skate, that's exercise!"

He waved her away, "Different sort, doesn't go uphill." He pointed upwards, "This shit though? You'd think that the entire world is actually on a slope."

"Just 'cause you're out of shape doesn't mean you're not going to keep up." Emily shuffled past him, "Otherwise we might leave you to be eaten by a bear."

He looked up at her with wide eyes, "There's no bears in Oregon... are there?"

"I don't know... *are there?*"

Grace rolled her eyes and stepped in, "Oregon has black bears, but the sign back there said that there's no known ones in the area. We should be fine if we stick to the trails anyway."

"Tsk, ruin my fun why don't you?" Emily grumbled as she bumped her shoulder, "I could've had him shaking for hours."

"I can think of better things to do with each other than be scared of bears crawling up our asses all night thank you very much."

"Oh? Like what?" Emily wiggled her eyebrows, Grace slapped her shoulder.

"Like camping you dumb perv!"

Eli raised his eyebrows, "Camping? Really?"

"I mean, yeah? Why not?"

"But... the bears..."

Grace grabbed his shoulders and shook, "There's no bears idiot, I literally just told you that!"

Emily thought it over; "We didn't bring the tent for nothing... And it would save us having to find a motel for tonight..." She smiled, "Sure, why not?"

Eli looked down the hill and slumped, "Does that mean we have to walk all the way back down there?"

"Well... Yeah. Unless you'd rather sleep on the ground with no covering and no warmth." She smirked, "And no protection from the bears."

"Alright fine!" He started jogging back down the hill, "We'll go get the stupid tent, I'm not letting some bear chew my ass off!"

Grace chuckled, throwing her arm around Emily, "You are a cruel, cruel woman Em."

"Yep, I am." She squeezed around Grace's hip, "But we should probably go help him."

"True, don't want him walking off alone and getting caught in some Blair Witch type shit."

They got to the car and back with the tent without incident, save for Eli slipping and falling into a pile of leaves, which left them all clutching at themselves in laughter. They found a quiet spot about twenty minutes up the hill, in a small clearing surrounded by trees and near a lake. The tent was set up and the sleeping bags placed inside, ready for when they decided to turn in. Grace decided to go off on her own for a little bit, walking a short distance away to try and get some candid nature shots without the danger of a second person destroying the atmosphere.

Which meant that Eli and Emily were left alone at the campsite to talk.

"I'm glad this is all going well, she looks like she's having a great time."

He smiled, "Tell me about it, everything's been awesome so far. Even this morning wasn't as weird as it could have been."

"Oh right, I... meant to talk to you about that..." She looked away, embarrassed.

He scratched his head, "What about it?" His eyes widened, "I didn't do anything did I?"

She waved her hands at him, "No! No you didn't do anything, well... intentionally..."

He tilted his head, "What does that mean?"

"Well... I woke up first, and we were all very close..." She looked down, "And, well... It was morning..."

His eyes widened in realization and his cheeks bloomed, "Oh god no! Oh, *I'm so sorry!*" He hid his face, "Christ that's embarrassing..."

"No, it's alright!" She reached out and grabbed his hand, "It's no big deal! Looking back it's kind of funny..." She ran her thumb over the back of his hand, they both locked eyes. Neither said anything, and neither looked away. Eventually the tension got to be too much, and they shuffled further away from each other. Mercifully, Grace chose that moment to show back up.

"Man, I got some great shots out there! I saw a baby deer, it was so cute!"

They both smiled at her, thankful for the distraction, "Come over here then, show us what the big deal is with a baby deer!"

She smiled and sat down in between them, the other two scooting in close to look over each of her shoulders. She went through each photo, explaining why she chose that particular angle, that moment, every little detail that went into taking her photos. They hung on to every word, only stopping when they noticed the sun was going down.

"I think that might be our cue to turn in, don't you think?"

Grace nodded, "Guess so, ready to squeeze our asses together again?"

"Oh I'm sure the tent isn't really that small on the inside," Eli looked over at the tent, "Is it?"

Emily giggled, "Eli it's the same tent we've always used, it's fucking tiny! I'll be surprised if we don't end up on top of each other out of necessity."

Grace stood, "Well, may as well get it over with. Who's going where?"

"I was in the middle last night, I think you should be there tonight."

She smirked, "Oh lucky me."

Emily grinned at Eli, "You might want to face away from her tonight though."

"What does that mean?" Grace looked at his rapidly reddening cheeks, her jaw dropped, "Oh dude! Come on, you didn't!"

"It's a biological occurrence ok? I can't help it!"

"Oh, she's right, you are definitely facing away from me."

"Argh!" He looked to the sky, "I hate the both of you!"

Emily snorted as she clapped him on the back, "Love you too Eli."

The sleeping situation wasn't nearly as awkward this time around, their arms naturally sweeping around each other as if they belonged there. Eli wasn't used to being the little spoon, but he couldn't find it in himself to complain because he didn't want a repeat of their first morning, but mainly because he couldn't deny how safe it felt.

And anyway, none of them were complaining about the additional warmth they were getting on that cold Oregon night. The temperature dropped lower and lower through the night, but none of them ever noticed, the only thing clear to them being the feelings of their hearts beating so close to one another, the soothing sound of their soft breathing in the night.

"H-hey, guys?" Grace's voice was tentative, like she didn't want to break the spell that they were under, "Are you awake?"

They both shifted, perking their heads up but not moving away, "Yea Gray? What's up?"

She smiled to herself, "Nothing really. Just wanted to say I love you guys."

The tent was silent, then the sound of movement as they snuggled in closer to her.

"We love you too Grace."

Chapter Five

Even though they knew she was kidding, the thought of bears finding them was enough to worm under their skin and make them get up bright and early. The sun had barely risen before the tent was taken down and packed up, the three of them making their way to the car.

"You and your big mouth Emily..." Grace tutted, "We could've been sleeping in for way longer if you hadn't said all that shit about the bears."

"Oh come on, how was I supposed to know it would bother us that much?"

Eli grunted, "How about the years that we've spent watching horror movies together and not being able to sleep at night?"

Emily huffed as she trudged down the path, "Fine, I get it. Dick move on my part."

"It's fine," Grace smirked as she nudged her with her elbow, "Eli's snoring would've scared off any bears anyway."

"I don't snore!" He looked outraged, but it rapidly faded to confusion, "Do I?"

Emily snorted, "Like a fucking chainsaw." He didn't, but why waste an opportunity for fun?

"I can't believe you're doing this to me. Me!" He put his hand on his chest, "My own best friends would hurt me like this!"

"Oh, get over it, you get to pick where we have breakfast today, how's that sound?"

He perked up, "Wow, you guys really are the best friends I could hope for, aren't you?"

They reached the car not long afterwards, the gear packed away and Emily taking the driver's seat. Eli squeezed in the back with Grace, her feet immediately going over his lap and his head leaning back in the seat. Emily looked back at them and smiled, "So Eli, where'd you wanna go?"

He yawned, "Uhh, I dunno... Something New Orleans-y."

"*New Orleans-y*?" She raised an eyebrow, "El I don't even know what a New Orleans breakfast *looks* like, what makes you think they sell them around here?"

"I read somewhere that there's literally thousands of food trucks in Portland, there's bound to be one for New Orleans, right?"

Grace snorted, "I mean, 'Bound to be' is a bit strong, but the chances aren't terrible."

Emily rubbed her eyes, "Fine. We will drive around and look for New Orleans breakfast food trucks, and when we fail in that we're going to have waffles. How's that sound?"

"Long as they have blueberry waffles."

"Screw your blueberry waffles."

"I cannot believe we found a fucking New Orleans food truck in like, five minutes." Emily took a bite out of the breakfast Po-Boy she decided on ordering, "Goddamn if this isn't good though."

Eli nodded with a mouthful of beignet, "Best idea I ever had."

"Even better than the road trip?" Grace leaned over and took a bite of a beignet, "Scratch that, this is the best idea you ever had."

Emily wiped her mouth, "So what do you guys wanna do today? We've got all day before we have to worry about finding somewhere to sleep, Portland's our oyster!"

"This might sound nerdy," Grace started, "But do you guys wanna go see the Science Museum?"

"You're right, that does sound nerdy." Eli grinned, "Let's do it then, science is pretty neat."

"'Science is pretty neat'?" Emily giggled, "That's the whitest shit you've ever said in your life."

He wrapped his arm around her neck, tickling her side, "Well I'm sorry we can't all be 100% super cool like you Em!"

She laughed and tried to squirm away from his hands, "No! Get off me you... you fucker!" She grabbed his hand with hers, and it was like the world slowed down again. It was the same feeling as last night, like electricity was being passed between them. She looked up into his eyes and she could tell that he was feeling it too, his expression both open and slightly panicked, as though he wasn't sure what this meant.

Emily knew what this meant, and it absolutely petrified her. Just as quickly as it started, it ended, Grace throwing herself into the middle and tackling them both to the ground. The three of them collapsed in a laughing heap, their chests heaving with mirth. The owner of the food stall wasn't nearly as impressed though, "Hey, you three! Either buy another sandwich or stop dicking around on my property!"

Grace got to her feet, "Don't worry dude, we were just getting out of here." She reached down, helping Eli to his feet with a grunt. She held her hand out for Emily, and when she took it she felt the exact same shock, though Grace's expression didn't change at all.

Though to have the same feeling for both her friends... What the hell could that mean?

The Science Museum was just as good as they hoped it would be, the three of them laying back in the planetarium and watching the lasers paint a story in front of them. Or at least,

Emily was trying to watch the lasers. Her friends on either side of her kept bumping into her, and what would normally be brushed off as little errant touches were making it very hard to focus now. Eli's hand brushing hers, Grace's leg briefly sliding against her own, it was all forcing her mind into overdrive and her emotions into damn near panic. While she knew they didn't mean anything by it, it couldn't be denied that it was having an effect on her, and she spent the majority of the laser show in a state of constant self-control. The last thing she needed was to weird her friends out by squeaking or doing anything else embarrassing when they so much as brushed her or breathed in her direction.

Unfortunately, she had no idea what to say when they stepped out of the planetarium, so she had to play dumb and pretend that the entire thing went over her head, not that she couldn't find it in herself to stay focused. They were none the wiser however, both talking excitedly about where they wanted to go next, and she found that to be a conversation that was much easier to engage in.

"How about the Japanese Gardens? There's bound to be at least one good photograph you can take there, right?" Emily placed her hand on Grace's shoulder, lingering for what even she thought was a second too long. Grace didn't seem to mind though.

"Great idea Em!" She turned and gave an absolutely dazzling grin, "Maybe you should drop the College thing and come help me out, you're pretty good at scouting apparently!"

She chuckled, "I'll think about it Gray."

"And leave me all alone in San Fran?" Eli shook his head dramatically; "I knew you'd forsake me like this Em!"

Emily scoffed, "Please, you'd see enough of me anyway without my ass always being in the apartment."

Grace raised an eyebrow, "You two were going to live together?"

They both looked at each other, Emily shrugged, "I mean, we were both thinking about it. Originally, we were thinking of it being the three of us, but now we're gonna have to definitely pair up." She whistled, "San Francisco is expensive."

She huffed, "Man, I'm going to miss out on so much shit when you guys move away."

Eli put his hand on her shoulder, rubbing it encouragingly, "Well I mean, we're not going to try and change your mind. But you could always change your mind."

She nodded, "I guess that's what this trip is all about right? Remembering how good it is to be together." She smiled softly at them, "Well, whatever. Let's go to the gardens."

The gardens weren't exactly exciting, but then again that wasn't really the point of the whole trip. Instead, hanging back and watching Grace absorb every detail of the gardens, and analyze each angle with a keen gaze, Eli and Emily realized that there needed to be more of this calmness in the trip. The excitement that they originally thought the trip would be was still going to be sought, but something as simple as sitting and watching the breeze work its way through the leaves was not going to be neglected.

Though it was certainly going to be balanced out.

"God, you guys! You know what we should do?" Grace bounced over to them, her camera being tucked away safely in its bag, "You know how we should spend tonight?"

"Umm, what exactly?" Emily felt she knew the answer, but didn't want to assume.

"We should get drunk!"

Yep, exactly what she thought it was.

So that was how they ended up, at some half nightclub, half dive bar combo in southern Portland, each of them four drinks deep and not looking to stop anytime soon. Grace hung her arms over both of her friends, slurring her speech, "You guys... I love you two so much! I'm going to miss you when you go!" Emily giggled and stroked the arm over her shoulder, "We won't be that far away! San Fran's like... twelve hours away? We can make that drive!"

Eli giggled, "I mean... we'll be tired as shit, and probably spend most of the time back asleep, but we can make that."

"Oh, you guys!" She squeezed them in, her drink coming perilously close to spilling from its glass, "I couldn't wish for better friends than you!" She slunk her arms lower and found their hands, "Come on, let's go dance!"

They couldn't do anything but laugh as they were dragged to the laughably small dance floor, some high energy song making them immediately start swaying their bodies as well as their drunken state would allow. They each remained close, so close that they could feel each other's breathing, the movement in their chests speeding up as they continued. Grace passed herself between each of them, one second her back pressed against Eli's chest, the next her arms were wrapped around Emily's neck, her head tucked securely in the crook of her neck. She didn't know how Eli felt about it, but Emily couldn't deny that it was having an effect on her, even if it wasn't Grace's intention. Eventually however, Grace pulled away from them, a quick swig of her drink being the only moment she took her eyes from them.

"I'm just gonna go get a refill, maybe sit down for a bit." She smiled at them, "You guys keep going though, I'll be back in a bit." And with that she walked off, the bar calling to her.

They both stared after her for a second before continuing, glasses placed down next to them and their eyes fixed on each other. Their movements were sloppy, no rhythm, but they were just what felt natural. As the music went on, and they started to step closer to each other, they got more fluid, started to move and sway with more ease. It wasn't long before they came into contact with each other, hands tentatively reaching out and touching arms, sweeping over hips. Each point of contact was like a shock of electricity, that same feeling going through her body like a runaway train, she looked up and could tell that he felt the same way, his eyes wide and his pupils blown wide from alcohol and... something else.

She reached a shaking hand up, brushing against his shoulder at first before resting against his cheek. He did the same, her head instinctively leaning into the contact. She closed her eyes and sighed to herself, feeling so utterly at peace that she could barely comprehend anything else around her. She brushed her thumb along his cheek and opened her eyes, seeing the gentle smile on his face. Neither of them realized that they were moving forward until their lips came into contact.

At first it was just a brush, a shock to the system that almost sent them reeling at the contact. They pushed forward, tentative pecks and awkward giggling giving way to something more. She captured his bottom lip between hers, sucking down and making him gasp. She took advantage of the surprise, slipping her tongue between his open lips and groaning at the feeling. His hands fell to her hips, his fingers squeezing tightly and pulling her into him. She reached around behind his head and grasped a handful of hair, tugging lightly on it as she explored his mouth, their minds almost gone in their singular pursuit. Eli sucked on her tongue, and she moaned, her body feeling like it was entirely aflame. Her head was cloudy, her pace getting more frantic as the seconds ticked by. When he pulled back and lowered himself to her neck, her pulse was going wild, her heart desperately trying to beat its way out of her chest. He attached his mouth to her pulse point, she whimpered. When he bit down her eyes flew open and she threw herself away.

She looked at him with sheer panic in her eyes, and he in his. "What... What the fuck are we doing?"

He covered his mouth with his hand, "I... I-I don't...." He looked to the side, his expression immediately dropping, "Oh fuck."

Emily looked as well, and the sight made her heart drop. Grace was standing there, drink long forgotten next to her as she watched on, mouth agape and eyes wide. The sight would have been hard enough to see, even if tears weren't flowing down her cheeks. Without another word, she stood and ran to the exit, the door almost flying off its hinges in her bid to escape.

"Fuck!" They followed her as fast as they could... it took less than a second before they found her. She was slumped over next to the wall, and though they couldn't see her face, it was obvious that she was still crying. They walked up cautiously, Emily extending her hand, "Grace... Hey, we're so-"

"How long's it been going on?" She looked at them, anger plain on her face, "How long have you been together?"

Eli jumped in, "We're not... It's not like that!" He shook his head, "I... We don't know what happened."

She scoffed, "You could've fooled me the way you were in there..."

Emily hung her head, "We're sorry Grace. This... This wasn't cool."

"No. It wasn't." She turned and started walking, "Whatever, I'm going back to the motel."

"Grace wait!" She paused, Emily continued, "Please, let us come with you. I know you're pissed but... we don't want anything to happen to you."

She didn't answer for a moment, then sighed, "Fine."

The motel they'd found before going out drinking was only two blocks away, but the walk felt like an eternity. None of the friends were looking at each other, whether it be from anger, guilt, or something else still remaining. The check-in was swift, a request for a room for three leading to one with two beds and a couch.

Eli insisted on the couch, but Emily wasn't going to let him. She couldn't help but blame herself for what was happening, one of her best friends confused by her, and the other quite possibly hating the both of them. As she tucked her body awkwardly under the blanket, Emily fought the tears that threatened to emerge, but she wouldn't let them. She wasn't the one who deserved to cry right now.

It was a long time before any of them slept, and none of them slept well that night.

Chapter Six

Unfortunately for all three of them, the amount of alcohol they drank was enough to give them a hangover, but not erase their memories of the previous night. So when they woke up, there was no denying how tense the room became on all sides, a thick cloud of regret covering them all. Emily got up from the couch, taking a second to pop her joints back in place before tentatively walking over to Grace's bed. She was sitting up, tightly wrapped in the covers, her eyes watching her every step of the way.

"Hey Grace." Emily sat down slowly, a nervous smile. She thought about placing her hand on her knee, but thought better of it once she saw the redness around her eyes. She sighed, "Look... What me and Eli did...What we did was shitty, and I'm sorry."

Eli got up from his own bed and shuffled over, his face pinched with regret as well, "I'm sorry too. I just..." He grabbed the sides of his head, "God, I wasn't thinking straight. Neither of us was."

He took a seat on the other side of Grace, Emily cautiously leaned forward. When she didn't pull away, Emily took it as her cue to pull her into a careful hug.

"We're so, so sorry Grace. You have every right to be pissed at us. This was supposed to be a trip about you, a big sendoff where we can all be together and..."

Eli took over, "And we fucked it up."

Grace shook her head, "No it's... It's fine." She smiled, too shaky to be completely genuine, "I overreacted, it's no big deal. If... if you guys want to be together then that's fine..."

Emily and Eli looked at each other, shaking their heads, "That's not happening it's just..." Emily sighed, "Look, we were shitfaced. Completely and utterly. We just got caught up in the moment is all."

She reached forward and squeezed Grace's hand, "We're not getting together, we're not going to just... leave you behind if that's what you're worried about."

She started to tear up all over again, Emily and Eli wrapped themselves around her. She shook her head through the tears, "I'm just being stupid. Can we... can we just get going? I just want to forget this."

They pulled back, looking at each other worriedly. Eli ran a hand down his face, "Sure thing, we should be on the road in ten."

Grace was already in the car when the others stepped out to leave, sitting in the middle of the back seat staring forwards. Eli was about to join her when Emily pulled him back, "Hey, we need to talk."

He groaned, "Fuck, I knew this had to happen sooner or later." She smiled sympathetically, "Yeah it sucks but... well, we really hurt her last night."

He nodded, "She says she's fine but come on, it's obvious she's not." He shook his head, "What the fuck was that last night? What was I thinking?"

"It wasn't just your fault." She sighed, "I remember being pretty active in it too."

"But why? Why'd we decide to do it all of a sudden?" He threw his arms up, "We've been drunk around each other for years! What changed?"

"Like I said before, I think we just got caught up in the moment, we were drunk, everything was exciting..." She shook her head, "Fuck, just be glad it didn't go any further. I don't know if she'd ever speak to us again."

"Yeah, I wouldn't blame her." Eli checked his watch, clucking his tongue in frustration, "Well, enough of that I guess. We need to get going. Long day ahead of us."

If the situation was awkward before, in the confines of the car it could be comparable to hell. Eli insisted on sitting in the back with Grace, Emily taking the wheel until they reached Salem. The backseat was an uncomfortable affair; Grace sitting as far on the left as she could... the thought of lying across the seat and against her friend was the furthest thing from her mind. Eli himself was sitting straight as a rod in his seat, afraid to even breathe for fear of making something worse. He and Emily almost jumped when the silence was broken.

"So how long are we driving today?" Grace's tone was bored, listless, though she was still making the effort to at least try and engage them. Even though she didn't want to be, she was still angry with both of them, but could tell that they were genuinely sorry.

Emily cleared her throat; "I looked it up before, San Francisco's about ten hours away by now."

"Fuuuuck." She let her head fall back, "We're gonna be on the road for *ten hours*?"

"Well I mean, we're gonna pull over at some point." Eli stretched, "No fucking way am I going to sit in a car for ten straight hours."

"Besides," Emily said, the hints of a smile in her voice, "We'll be stopping in Salem in about twenty minutes."

"Oooo, spooky." Grace let herself smile, "Wonder if they'll put me on a stake."

Eli raised his hand, "I hate to burst your bubble guys, but it's not the same Salem."

They both looked at him, "What?"

"We're gonna stop in Salem, Oregon." He held up his phone, "The witch trials were in Salem, Massachusetts."

Emily thumped her hand against the dashboard, "Why the fuck would they have two Salem's?"

"Why wouldn't they change that?" Grace rubbed her temple, "Why would you still have your town be called Salem after that?"

"Salem, Oregon fucking sucks." Emily scowled, "I hate it already."

"Just wanted to see some witches..." Grace crossed her arms and huffed, "This is crap."

"Bet there's nothing cool that ever happened there."

Eli tapped Emily's shoulder, "One Flew Over the Cuckoo's Nest was filmed there, that's something at least."

She took a moment to consider, then sighed, "Fine, that's pretty cool."

Sensing that some of the awkwardness was fading, Eli pressed on, "So Grace," He nudged her, "I brought my board along. Wanna catch some pictures of me scaring some old people?"

She laughed, an actual, full-bellied laugh, "The only way you're gonna scare them is by falling off and smacking your nuts on a parked car." She grinned, "Hell yeah, I'm in."

Inwardly, Emily breathed a sigh of relief. Maybe things weren't going to be so bad after all.

Salem was, as unfortunately predicted, completely witch-free. While Grace was able to get some good photos, the State Capitol Building being a favorite spot, no doubt because Eli bailed and hit his back on almost every surface, the city as a whole just wasn't what they were looking for. The people were nice enough, but after a half hour they were more than ready to leave.

"Well," Emily sighed as she got in the back seat with Grace, "Aside from Eli totaling himself that was disappointing." Grace hummed in agreement, "Maybe if we knew there weren't gonna be any witches we would've enjoyed it more. Food for thought I guess."

"Well I'll tell you what they do have though." Eli buckled himself in as he started the car, "A gas station, which is good because we're almost running on fumes."

"Wait, what?" Emily leaned over the seat and stared at the gas level, "Fuck, did we just keep forgetting? Could swear it was a full tank when we left."

He shrugged, "I mean, we've been driving a lot. Like, we're over two hundred miles away from Seattle now."

"Holy shit, really?" Grace was leaning over her seat now, her eyes wide, "Seriously? We've come that far already?"

"Yep, and by the end of today..." He pulled out his phone and double-checked on the GPS, "It'll be over eight hundred."

"That is so cool." She sat back, then a second later kicked the back of his seat, "Well what are we waiting for? Fill it the hell up and let's go!"

Emily joined in, "Yeah let's go! We've still got like... nine more hours of driving or something."

"Nine more?" Grace pursed her lips, "Jeez. What are we gonna do for nine whole hours?"

She shrugged, "Cards?"

Grace blew a raspberry; "Yeah sure, we'll play go fish for nine hours. Try again Em."

"Alright then chuckles, we'll just sit here and talk the whole time. How's that sound?"

"Like agony."

Eli raised an eyebrow, pulling into the gas station, "Wait, but all we do is talk? Why's it agony now?"

"Because when we usually talk it's because I want to. Now it'd be because we need something to do, takes all the fun out of it."

"Hmm, I get what you're saying." He made eye contact through the rear-view mirror and smirked, "You're an idiot."

"If you weren't pumping gas I'd kick your ass!"

"Oh. My. Fucking. God." Grace rolled her eyes into the back of her skull, "This is taking so long! I forgot how much of this country is... well... country!"

"Tell me about it, the trees and stuff are pretty but... something to break it up wouldn't be so bad."

"I dunno, just think about it this way, how many of those kids we knew in high school are still sitting in Seattle?" Eli shrugged, "Most of 'em probably, right?"

They both nodded, "Yeah, a lot of them are locals."

"Exactly! Look at how far we've come in three days! Those other kids are sitting at home, not doing anything!" He laughed and thumped his fist against the roof, "Suck it losers! We're taking over this goddamn country!"

His enthusiasm was infectious, and soon Grace and Emily found themselves whooping at the top of their lungs, windows rolled down and screaming into the forest. Somehow that enthusiasm carried them through the next three hours of their ride, only starting to wane just before they reached their next stop.

"Well, time for a rest!" Eli looked at the welcome sign, "Welcome to..." He did a double take, "Weed, California?"

"You're shitting me." Emily leaned forward and took a close look at the sign herself, "Holy crap there really *is* a town called Weed. This is California all right." She turned to Grace, "Ready?"

She lifted her camera to her eye and smirked, "I was born for this tourist shit."

The three of them stepped out, Emily and Eli taking up position in front of the sign. After setting up her camera on the hood of the car and setting the timer, Grace joined them. They each struck a pose as the camera went off, just managing to contain their laughter at how stupid the situation was, and how stupid the picture itself was going to look.

"Alright, now that that's done we can go get some lunch. Or early dinner. Whatever." Grace collected her camera and got back in the car.

"Well who knows," Emily turned to Eli, "With a name like this it's gotta be more interesting than Salem, right?"

"Holy crap there is no one in this town!" Eli looked from side to side as they drove up the main road, the streets practically deserted.

"Well a quick search shows this place has just over two thousand residents." Emily looked over her phone to the road, "I'm pretty sure we passed more people on the road getting here."

"Should be easy to find a place to eat then right?" Grace peered through the windows, sweeping both sides of the street, "A small town like this has to have a diner of some sort."

"You'd think so..." Eli spotted the corner and smiled, "And you'd be right!" He pulled over to the side and parked, "You guys ready for some country food?"

"It's a small town. Not a farm Eli."

He waved his hand as he got out of the car, "Same thing, don't lie."

They stepped inside, their eyes immediately being drawn to the deer head on the wall. Grace chuckled as they sat down, "I feel like I'm in a Twin Peaks episode."

"Well I hate to bust that fantasy, but we've only got time for a coffee and some waffles, then we're heading off again." Emily shrugged, "Maybe two servings of waffles."

"Eh, I'll take it."

Grace leaned back after they ordered, her eyes fixed on Emily, "So, Em... I wanted to ask something..."

"Hmm?" Emily raised an eyebrow, "What's up?"

"Why'd you break up with Christy?" Emily's eyes widened, Grace put her hands up, "Not to like, interrogate you or anything like that, you two just seemed to... fit, you know?" She sighed, "Aside from the fact that we were in high school and that shit never lasts?"

Grace smirked, "Yes, aside from that."

"I dunno... It... She was nice, we're still friends but she wasn't..." She fought to cover her mouth in realization. *She wasn't either of you.*

"S-She uhh... we were just too different in some ways."

Eli nodded, "It happens. Me and Lee? Same thing."

"Man..." Grace whistled, "High school sucks."

"Don't have to tell me twice."

Emily shook her head.

It was infinitely less confusing though.

It was getting late by the time they crossed into San Francisco, but none of them could hide their excitement.

"Welcome to San Francisco! One of the gayest places in the world!" Eli smiled ear to ear as they drove further and further in.

Emily laughed next to him, "My people!" She smiled as she watched the streets pass by, "Can you believe we'll be living here in a few months?"

"I know... It's insane."

They looked back at Grace, who was silent at their exchange. She had a small smile on her face though, so they weren't quite sure what to make of it. She looked up at them, "Don't worry about me, just thinking, you know?"

"Yeah," Emily nodded slowly, "Yeah, I know."

They found a cheaper hotel deeper in the city, the three of them once again requesting a room with two beds. Though they'd had a pretty enjoyable day, none of them were forgetting exactly how the previous night and the morning had been.

They stepped through the door, and Emily immediately moved to take the couch. Eli placed his hand on her shoulder, "Hey, come on. You took the couch last night, it's my turn now."

She shook her head, "It's my fault though..."

"Funny, because I think it's my fault." He smiled, "Let's agree to disagree."

She chuckled, shaking her head, "Fine, you win. Or lose, considering you're sleeping on a couch."

Eli jumped down and threw his legs up, "Yep, this sucks already." He closed his eyes, "Goodnight you guys."

"Night Eli," Grace turned to look at Emily from her bed, "Night Emily."

She nodded, drawing the covers over herself, "Night Grace." She lay awake for some time afterwards, thinking of her two friends. It was quite plain to see, no matter how much they denied it, that there was something between herself and Eli.

She'd given up on trying to deny that. But between her and Grace? She didn't like what her intuition was telling her, and was more than happy to deny it for now.

Unfortunately for her, her dreams weren't going to let her escape from those thoughts.

Chapter Seven

The morning, while nowhere near as awkward as the previous, was still not an ideal thing to wake up to. Looking around and seeing the different sleeping arrangements, the three couldn't do anything but remember exactly why they were sleeping separately in the first place, and with those memories came renewed feelings of guilt and jealousy, repressed though they wished them to be.

Pushing aside her own feelings, Grace was the first to speak up, "So, what's on the agenda for today? What's cool in San Francisco?"

Eli pulled out his phone and scrolled through some pages, "Well, says here the Fisherman's Wharf is great if you like fish and food. What do you say we go there?"

She nodded, "I'm down for it." She turned and looked at Emily, a question in her eyes, "How about you Em? In the mood for fish and food?"

Emily giggled at the rhyme, "Yeah, yeah that sounds great Gray. I'm fucking starved."

"Tell me about it," She lifted her arms above her head and stretched, "Turns out waffles aren't really much of a filling dinner, who would have thought?"

Emily didn't reply, her eyes were fixed on the line of Grace's stomach, a pale expanse of which had been exposed by her stretching. She tried to look away, but today of all days couldn't will herself. She was sure she was blushing furiously by the time Grace dropped her arms and covered her stomach again.

"You alright Em?" Grace tilted her head, a look of concern on her face, "You look really flushed, something wrong?"

She shook her head, "Yeah, yeah I'm fine just... probably still a little tired from the drive."

"You want to stay in? I mean, I'm fine with just taking it easy, how about you Eli?"

He nodded, "Yeah, no point in going out if all of us can't enjoy it."

"No, it's fine. Really, you guys, I'm *fine*." She smiled, "Let's get going! Could really go for some crab."

"Emily it's eleven in the morning."

She shrugged, "Every time is crab time."

The three of them walked down to the Wharf, the sights on the way astonishing to them. One thing they thought they knew but never fully realized is just how colorful San Francisco is, whole streets being covered in street art or occupied by dancers and artists. They thought that Seattle was arty, apparently, they had quite a bit of research to do.

"Wow this place is cool!" Emily walked along the wall, fingers brushing over a colorful mural celebrating the community, "It's like the city is alive!"

"Jesus, you'd think everyone who lived here was an artist..." Eli ran a hand over the mural, stepping over the parts that descended down onto the footpath, "Wait, is everyone who lives here an artist?"

"Not everyone..." Grace skipped through the streets, grinning at the dancers, "City has suits, just like any other. They're just harder to see through the brightness."

"Wow, that's... unexpectedly bitter of you Grace."

"Is it?" She put her finger on her chin in thought, "I think it's really beautiful though, that the art and culture is still the most visible part of the city, that that's what it's known for." She smirked, "I mean yeah, the suits suck but even I have to admit there's a purpose to them."

"'The suits have a purpose?' Who are you and what did you do to our Rebel Girl?" Emily gasped theatrically, "Are you a corporate plant? You have to tell us if you are!"

"Oh, shut up dork. I just mean that if it means this city can still be this vibrant, and this arty, and this beautiful... I guess I can tolerate the corporate side."

Eli pursed his lips, "Fair enough." He chuckled, "This trip really is changing us, isn't it? Little old Grace is finally making peace with modern society."

She slapped the back of his head, "I never said that Skater Boy."

"Oooo that reminds me, you think you could get some good shots of me on my board here?"

She snickered, "Why do you insist on still doing this to yourself? You fall on your ass every time I get my camera out and it looks like it hurts every time."

He sputtered, then suddenly blushed, "Honestly? Probably because you look like you're having a great time with it."

Emily did a double take, "That was... unexpectedly honest..."

Grace blushed as well, then shook her head, "You don't have to hurt yourself to let me have fun, you dumb ass. Now I feel like crap."

He stumbled "No! It's not your fault, how could you know?" He smiled to himself, "Besides, I gotta admit that they're good pictures. You really capture that look of agony on my face."

"After the amount of hits you've taken on railings I'd be shocked if you could still have kids."

He scratched the back of his neck, "I was uh, kinda worried about that myself for a while."

Grace and Emily raised their eyebrows at him, he waved his hands frantically, "No it's fine I went to a doctor! Little guys are fine, nothing wrong with them!"

Emily groaned, "I don't ever want to hear about your 'little guys' ever again."

Grace spoke from behind her hand, "I second that motion."

"Alright fine, no talk about my swimmers from now on."

The other two growled, advancing on him. He promptly raised his hands in surrender, "Alright, alright I get it. Not funny, gotcha."

They took their seats on the boardwalk, takeaway seafood in their hands. They sat back and sighed, looking to the sky in their relaxation. They let the tension bleed out of their bodies, so content that they couldn't even find it in themselves to be awkward over touching each other right now. They just wanted to sit back, and put themselves in a state of pure contentment. Unlike so many of those times, this one went uninterrupted by either poor circumstances or time restrictions. Here they could just lay back, and let the sound of the water calm them to their cores. Emily yawned, her head falling on Grace's shoulder. She didn't see it, but it was the first time Grace blushed at their contact.

After about fifteen minutes of peaceful relaxation and near sleep, they decided that they should probably eat the food that they paid for. Emily eagerly dug into her crab, taking crab time very seriously. She groaned in delight at the flavor, the taste of the crab amazing and the texture to die for, almost melting in her mouth at contact. The others' orders didn't disappoint either, Eli's fried squid the right amount of salty and Grace's tempura wonderfully crispy.

"Guys, I think I'm in love with this city." Emily moaned around a mouthful, not even able to will herself to swallow first, "Seriously, this is so good."

"Tell me about it, you assholes have me seriously reconsidering whether or not to move here."

Eli chuckled, but brushed her shoulder, "Glad to hear, but remember what we said, only if you want to. We'll support you either way."

"Oh god, you just told me your boys were fine down there, you don't have to act like I'm your kid." Grace smirked at the look of indignation that crossed his face, before it transformed into almost hysterical laughter.

"Fu-fuck you, you're gonna make me choke on my squid!" She at least had the common courtesy to wait until he swallowed his food before she tackled him, capturing him in yet another headlock. "What are you gonna do without me huh?" She paused, "Wait, shit. What am I gonna do without *you*? Everything's gonna be so boring!"

"Well..." He tapped her arm, she loosened her grip, "I could stream myself skating to you? Give you a live stream of me falling over?"

She rolled her eyes, "I told you, you don't have to keep hurting yourself to give me a good time."

"Uhh..." He grimaced, "To be completely honest, it was only like 60% of the time that it was on purpose." He looked down in embarrassment, "Some of those tricks are hard."

She smiled and shook his head, "You dork, you're doing alright to me. When you don't bust your ass on the ground you look pretty cool." She leaned over and looked at Emily, "Isn't that right Em?"

She nodded, "Yeah, when you're not in horrific pain you look awesome." She smirked, "Even then sometimes."

"Aww thanks guys." He wiped a fake tear from his eye, "Makin' me choke up here."

"No, that's Grace."

"Oh, right. Get off me."

They walked along the shore, the Golden Gate Bridge looming ahead of them in the distance. They looked forward in wonder, seeing the way it spanned across the water, a marvel of engineering.

"Can you believe someone woke up one day and thought of that?" Grace shook her head in amazement, "Just think of all the stuff we take for granted now and imagine a time without it..."

Emily nodded, "Bridges, skyscrapers, Ziggy Stardust..." She ran a hand down her face, "It's insane. The world is only the way it is because insane people woke up and said, 'I'm going to mold the world.'"

"I know, just think..." Eli squinted, "Wait a minute, Ziggy Stardust?"

She nodded, "Yeah, think about how different music would be without him. Or Bowie's career in general."

"Nine Inch Nails, Saul Williams... I mean they probably would have come along eventually but they probably wouldn't be the same."

Grace chuckled, "I can't believe you nerds are going on about Bowie and Saul Williams right now."

Emily raised a finger in indignation, "They are two of the most important artists of the 20th and 21st centuries!"

"Yeah yeah, I've heard you say this before Em. You're still right, I'm not denying that." She leaned in and squeezed Emily's shoulder, "But drunk you really loves to talk about it. Like, a lot."

Emily crossed her arms, "Drunk me knows what she's talking about..."

Before they knew it, they'd reached the Golden Gate Bridge, the walkway stretching out in front of them, just begging them to start walking. Emily took her first steps, walking a few feet before realizing no one was following her. She turned around, seeing Eli standing off to the side, Grace tilting her head at him.

"Guys? Something wrong?" Emily stepped forward hesitantly.

Eli looked at Grace for a few more seconds then to her, smiling shakily, "Yeah, just dizzy you know. Think I'm gonna take a breather for a bit."

"Are you alright? Where do you wanna sit down?"

He shook his head, "It's fine, don't worry. You two go on ahead," He took one last look at Grace and immediately dropped his gaze, "Enjoy yourselves."

Emily was confused, but reached out her hand to Grace anyway, "Alright... come on Gray, let's get going..."

Grace followed after her, staring at Eli in confusion herself. Sudden realization came over her, and she had to fight the urge to gasp, her eyes going wide at the nod he gave her.

"No fucking way..." She whispered to herself, and was still staring when he turned his back and began to walk off. She jogged after Emily before she could lose her nerve.

Why would he...

She shook her head, it didn't matter why. What mattered was that he gave her a chance.

She wasn't going to let it be thrown away.

They walked together, almost shoulder to shoulder along the bridge, the San Francisco Bay stretching out around them, a seemingly endless expanse of water and city. In the distance they could see Alcatraz, and Emily couldn't resist.

"Your 'best'! Losers always whine about their best. Winners go home and fuck the prom queen."

Grace erupted in laughter, clutching at her stomach, "Your Sean Connery really needs work Em."

She shrugged, grinning herself, "I dunno, I think it's getting better. These things age like a fine wine after all."

Grace shook her head, "You are ridiculous, you know that right?"

"If that's what it takes to keep a smile on your face, I'm all for it." They both blushed, that was maybe a little more romantic than Emily was meaning for it to be.

It was a very good opportunity for Grace though.

"I think just being around you is enough to keep a smile on my face."

Emily snapped her head to her, "I... Grace?"

She swallowed nervously, the butterflies in her stomach well and truly beating their wings, "It's true you know. Being around you and Eli... It's the best thing in my life, even more than the photography." She chuckled, "And you know how much I fucking love photography."

Emily walked them over to the side of the bridge, leaning on the railing, "What brought this on? I mean I love hearing how much you care about us, don't get me wrong..." She giggled, "But I dunno, this seems really spontaneous." Outwardly she looked calm, like they were just having a simple conversation. Internally was a whole other matter, her heart going into overdrive at the very thought of what this conversation could be about.

"I guess you're right," Grace smiled, "We are a pretty affectionate group by default, aren't we?" She shook her head, "But this isn't like that it... It's more complicated."

Ok, now she was starting to panic. "Complicated how?" She reached out to Grace and threaded their hands together, "Come on, you can tell me, it's ok."

"It started when I saw you two kissing."

Emily squeezed her eyes shut, "God Gray I'm so sorry... We-" She was cut off when Grace pressed her finger against her lips, her eyes shot open in surprise.

"It's fine, it really is." She bowed her head, "I'm not gonna lie, it hurt at the time, but I didn't know why..." She looked up, their eyes meeting, "Now I do."

She ran her thumb along the back of Emily's hand, "I thought I was just worried. Worried that you two would leave me behind, forget about me, move on with your lives and build something without me. And yeah, that was definitely part of it, but I was scared to admit what it was really about."

Emily's words came out as a whisper, "What was it?"

She smiled, nervously, vulnerably, "I was jealous."

"J-Jealous?"

She nodded, "Mm-hmm. Of who, I wasn't sure. But when I think about losing you, losing either of you... It's something I can't stomach." She chuckled, "Honestly, looking back I can kinda see this stretching back for a while. Remember when you were going out with Hank?"

Emily giggled, "It lasted three weeks and the entire time you two gave him death glares!"

"Yeah," She smiled, "Makes sense now doesn't it?" She reached up and stroked Emily's cheek, she leaned into the contact. This was starting to feel familiar. "I just... Couldn't bear to see someone *else* with you..." She started to lean forward, "Now I know why."

Emily slipped her eyes closed and leaned forward, where Grace was waiting for her.

Chapter Eight

Emily's first thought was that her lips were warm, but there was another feeling underneath them. One not so easily summed up by a single emotion. Grace tasted like autumn, spices, smoke. She tasted like the first breath you take when you reach home after a long trip, like the feeling you get when you slip into a warm bath after walking for miles.

She couldn't help but groan into her, the kiss like the ultimate narcotic she'd been searching her whole life for, and now that she found it would gladly spend every waking moment imbibing. They slipped their arms around each other's waists, pulling the other closer and deepening their contact. Grace ran her hand delicately along Emily's cheek, so softly that it was like she was made of the finest of china, something so fragile that a stern look would shatter her.

Emily grabbed a fistful of her jacket at the same time as her tongue darted out, passing over her lips and requesting entry. Grace gladly obliged, moaning shamelessly at the feeling of the muscle beginning to explore her mouth. She fought back with her own, their tongues engaged in their own private battle, one that neither was certain whether or not they wanted to win at or not.

They pulled back for but a second, their foreheads resting against each other as they struggled to regain their breath. They dove back in without a second thought, Grace sinking her teeth into Emily's lower lip and tugging lightly. She almost saw stars at the feeling, her friend knowing just what to do at any given moment. It wasn't long before Emily's hand slipped lower, slinking around the back and lightly grasping at Grace's behind. She squeezed down, and the noise that Grace made would be seared into her brain and appearing in her dreams for eternity.

It was only after the favor was returned that her mind started to wonder. Thoughts of Eli, taking the place of Grace. Taking the place of her. She shook her head lightly to clear the thoughts, but couldn't force them away. Before she could suppress it, she whimpered, and Grace knew her well enough to know it wasn't made out of desire or happiness. She pulled back, dismayed to see tears rolling down her face.

"Emily..." She wiped a tear away, "Emily what's wrong?"

"I... Nothing... nothing's wrong." She sniffled, and couldn't help the next flood that came.

Grace shook her head sadly, "No, something's wrong, what is it?"

It was a few seconds of shaking before she could find it in herself to reply, "Everything. Everything's wrong, and I don't know what to do."

Grace shook her head and ran a hand up and down Emily's back, even as she felt her own heart breaking, "Is it Eli? Do you..." She sighed, "Are you in love with him?"

"No. It's not... it's not because of Eli." She pulled back and hugged herself.

Grace looked at her in desperation, "Then what is it? Please, tell me!"

Emily couldn't help but scream, "It's because of *both* of you! And I don't know what to do!"

Grace was taken aback, "*Both* of us? What do you..." Her eyes widened as Emily turned and sprinted off, "Emily! Emily wait!"

Emily was much faster than her, and it wasn't long before she lost sight of her. But even though she couldn't see her anymore, she could hear her sobs clear from where she stood. "Stupid. *Stupid*!" She ran until her lungs were like fire, until her legs felt like jelly and she was certain she was going to collapse. She stumbled forward until she found a bench on the side of the road, falling down onto it and sinking her head into her hands. She wept, openly, loudly, not caring who saw her doing it or how it made anyone else feel.

"You idiot. You stupid, dumb, horny fucking teenager!" She dug her nails into her palms, crescents indenting in the skin, "You just can't control yourself, can you? You have to leap at them without a second thought, don't you?"

She shook her head, trying to will the memories of their lips away. Trying to forget how it made her feel, how happy she was in the moment. Instead she remembered the look of anguish on Grace's face when she pulled away from Eli, tried to imagine the betrayal that he would feel knowing that she made a pass at her other best friend. "This is my punishment. I deserve this."

Her weeping began anew, crying until there were no more tears left to give and she was just shaking. She couldn't imagine how the others must feel, not just that she would cross a boundary like that with so little hesitation, but that she wasn't even brave enough to stay with them. Another sob wracked her body as she remembered the look of heartbreak on Grace's face just before she ran. "Oh my god, that's why Eli stayed behind..." She covered her face and screamed, even Eli had stepped up and tried to make them both happy, and what did she do with

70

that chance? She fumbled it, she ruined it, she did nothing except hurt her two best friends, cause them betrayal and heartbreak. Emily shook her head, "I'm a terrible friend, and I'd be a terrible partner... I just lost them both." Her lip quivered, "Why? Why did this have to happen?" She sunk even lower into the bench, almost touching the ground.

"Why did I have to fall in love with both of them?"

She shook her head, too despondent to do anything else, "This whole trip was one big mistake. One big, selfish attempt to try and have them be around me one last time." She shrugged, "What else could it possibly be? You selfish fucking idiot."

She sighed, looking upwards at the sky.

It wasn't nearly as comforting as it was an hour ago.

"Come on, come on!" Grace listened to the ring of the phone, "Pick up your fucking phone Eli!"

After what seemed an eternity, he answered, voice clear, if not slightly bored, "Yo, Gray. What's up?"

She stopped, sighed to herself. Even now, thinking of it she had to will herself not to cry, "Emily ran off."

She almost heard him straighten up, "Wait, what? Why would she run off?"

"She was confused about me, and about you. I asked her if she was in love with you, if that was why she was so rattled." She paused, "She said it was because of the both of us."

"Ok, ok. What way did she run off?" He shook his head, "Please don't tell me it was further along the bridge..."

"No, no she ran back the way we came, she probably almost ran right past you."

"Are you on your way back as well?"

She nodded, "Yeah, I'm running back as we speak."

"Alright, I'll wait here for you. We'll look for her together."

"Thanks Eli." She grimaced, debating whether to tell him or not. Honesty won, "Hey El?"

"Yeah? What's up Gray?"

She stopped, trying to will the words out. She forced them past her lips, "I kissed Emily."

The line was silent for a long time, she was afraid that he would just end the call, not speak to her. She was wrong, "...That doesn't matter. What matters is that we find her and make her feel safe." He smiled, "That's what friends are for right?"

Grace exhaled, releasing the tension that she wasn't even aware she'd been holding onto, "Yeah, that's what friends are for."

Emily didn't know how long she'd been sitting there staring at nothing, it could have been minutes, it could have been hours. But when she heard those familiar voices, voices that she would recognize even if she didn't hear them for decades, she felt as though she was ready to break all over again. She didn't move an inch, not even when Eli slid into the seat next to her and wrapped his arm around her shoulders. Not even when Grace took a seat on her other side and did the exact same.

"I fucked up." Their heads shot up at her words, brows furrowed in concern.

"What? No, Em, you didn't..." She cut off Eli before he could continue, not wanting to hear him make excuses for her.

"Come on, I made out with you not even three days ago. You saw how much it hurt Grace." She shook her head, "And today I did the exact same thing to you."

Grace squeezed her shoulder, "Emily, I kissed you first. That's on me."

"Yeah, and I went right along with it. And I enjoyed it!" She scoffed, "Of course I enjoyed it, why wouldn't I? I'm just that selfish apparently."

72

"Alright, that's it." She looked at Eli, who for the first time looked furious. Though not for the reasons she was expecting, "I'm not going to sit here, and watch you badmouth yourself. You know what I think about you kissing Grace?"

She shrunk, ready for the verbal onslaught, "What?"

He stood and threw his hands up, "I don't fucking care!"

She looked up, confused, "But... I thought you..."

"Was attracted to you? Yeah, I am! But who cares?" He knelt down, squeezing her hand between his, "I am your friend first and foremost, that comes before everything. I saw the way you looked at Grace, and I saw the way she looked at you. It wasn't even a decision."

Even Grace was surprised, "But didn't it hurt? To step back like that?"

"Yeah, it did. But it would have been worth it." He smiled, "If you two got to be happy, if our group got to stay together, even if it meant that I had to be a little alone every now and then, it would've been worth it. You two mean the most in the world to me."

Grace nodded, "I... I was being selfish before." She turned to Emily, "I realized after you ran off... I don't want you gone from my life. Even if you got together with dickhead here," Eli slapped her arm, "I would have endured it. I'd give anything to have you back."

"But with the way I feel about the both of you..." Emily shook her head, "Normal people don't feel this way..."

"So you care about more than one person, how does that make you a bad person?" Grace made her look into her eyes, "You are far from a bad person Em. You are one of the most selfless, caring people I have ever known, and I'm fucking honored to call you my friend." She smiled gently, squeezing one of

Emily's hands, "Even if you care for the both of us, even if you love the both of us... Even if you make a decision..."

Eli squeezed her other hand, "And even if you don't..."

"We'll be there for you, every step of the way."

He nodded, "Because that's what friends are for."

She felt her eyes welling up again, her chuckle coming out far more wet than she thought it would, "God you guys I... I don't know what..." She sighed, collapsing into their arms, "I'm so fucking exhausted."

Grace laughed, "I can imagine. What do you say we get you back to the hotel?"

She nodded, slinging her other arm around Eli's shoulder, "That sounds good. I..." The words got caught in her throat, "Thanks you guys."

Eli shrugged, "Don't worry about it, consider it payback for all the times you've been there for us."

"Does it really balance out?"

Grace shook her head, "Not even close, we still owe you big time."

They didn't bother getting into separate beds this time, knowing that Emily felt more alone than ever, despite how their talk went. They climbed into the same bed, Emily in the middle, their arms wrapping securely around her. She almost teared up at the familiar warmth, that much needed closeness, but she had been right before. She was exhausted.

She was out like a light before she could count to ten.

When she woke it was to the feeling of one pair of arms around her. A quick glance confirmed two things, that it was Grace who almost had her in a death grip, and that it was two o'clock in the morning. She looked around blearily, wondering where Eli was, before she shivered from the breeze. The balcony door was open, the curtain blowing into the room, Eli clearly visible behind it. She carefully extracted herself from Grace's arms, thankful not for the first time that she was such a heavy sleeper. She missed the warmth immediately, but knew that she had to see if Eli was ok.

It wasn't just a heavy day for her after all.

Emily knocked on the door frame, "Hey, Eli... You ok?"

He turned in surprise, exhaling a lungful of smoke, "Oh shi-"

He chuckled, "Yeah, yeah I'm fine."

"Are you sure?" She pointed at the cigarette in his fingers, "Because you only ever smoke when you're stressed the fuck out."

He looked at his hand, then huffed out another laugh, "Jesus, you know me so well don't you?" He pointed next to him, "Well, have a seat I guess."

She sat in the seat next to him, eagerly taking the cigarette when he offered, "Been a rough day huh?"

"Yeah, for you more than anyone."

"Don't give me that." She shook her head, "I know for a fact it's been hard on you both. Hell, these last few days have been hard on you two."

"We meant what we said before though, no matter what, we're with you."

She smiled, squeezing his knee, "You two are the best friends I could ask for, you know that right?"

Eli nodded, his expression somewhat distant, "Yeah, we do. Besides..." He sighed, "I kind of understand what you're going through."

She was confused for a second, before her eyes widened, "You don't mean..."

He looked through the door, gaze fixed on a sleeping Grace, "Yeah, I do mean."

Emily leaned in, lowering her voice, "Does she know?"

"No. If she did I think we'd all be going through mental breakdowns." He sighed, shaking his head, "I don't even know if there's a fucking word for what this is, other than confusing."

She giggled, "Fucking tell me about it. I thought I was going insane." She reached out, putting her arm hesitantly around his shoulders, "It... feels nice. Knowing someone else is going through the same thing."

"Yeah..." He nodded, before standing, "We should probably head back in, before she gets cold."

"You want to go on her other side or...?"

He shook his head, smiling softly at her, "No, it was fine the way it was before." He held out his hand, after a second's hesitation she took it, following him back to the bed.

Chapter Nine

The bed was warm, comforting. For the first time in a few days all three of them woke up with no apprehension, no guilt, no anger. Just a feeling of contentment, of safety. Emily looked from side to side, blinking the sleep from her eyes, a small smile on her face.

Grace and Eli looked at her, noticeably nervous about how she would feel since last night. She squeezed them close, whispering into the air, "A little longer. Can we just enjoy this for a little longer?"

They smiled to themselves, slinking their arms deeper around her, "Sure thing Em. As long as you want."

By the time they got up it was almost two in the afternoon, the breeze blowing lightly over the bed and slowly waking them again. They each sat up and stretched, joints popping as they adjusted to their new positions. "Wow," Grace groaned as she leaned back, "Finally, a good night's sleep."

"Tell me about it." Eli didn't look at her for much longer than a second, something that Emily realized had been happening for a while.

She nudged them both with her elbow, "How about we go get some more food then get on the road? LA awaits after all."

"Hell yea! I think I saw a place that served Bouli... Bola..."

Grace shook her head to herself, "Some fucking seafood soup thing!"

"Bouillabaisse." Eli nodded, "My mom made it for me once. It's delicious, you'll love it."

"I seriously wanna stay here forever, just eat on that boardwalk for the rest of the year." She shrugged and got up, pulling her pants on, "But it's whatever. Some seafood soup will have to do for now."

"Bouillabaisse."

"You know I'm never going to be able to say that, stop trying."

"You know..." Grace slurped her soup loudly, trying to distract them from her thinking, "I really could see myself living here one day." She spoke quickly before they could reply, "Nothing to do with my final decision so far, just putting it out there, you know?"

"For the last time Gray," Emily leaned over, squeezing her shoulder; "We'll support you no matter what, ok?"

"I know it's just... after last night..." She looked up apologetically, Emily sighed.

"What happened last night should have nothing to do with how you live your life." She shrugged, "If we move away, and we don't see you as often will that hurt? Yeah, it will." Emily smiled, reaching for her hand, "But it would make me fucking miserable if you decided to give up on chasing what you really wanted to try and make us happy."

Grace shook her head, "Fuck, we've gotta stop having these serious conversations when we're eating."

Eli snorted, tossing his empty packaging into the bin, "Hey, you started it this time." He looked down at them, "But I think that after last night..." He took a deep breath, letting it out slowly, "I think we should sit down and have a talk tonight, really lay our shit on the table. Now's the time for us to be completely honest with each other."

The others were clearly nervous, but nodded. "Yeah, yeah I agree. It's not fair for Emily to be the only one, I need to get some stuff off my chest as well."

"Well alright then." He held his hands out, pulling them to their feet, "Let's get to LA then, faster we do this the better."

"So... What's in LA then?" Grace leaned against Emily, "Something cool that you guys wanna go see?"

They shrugged, Emily explained, "Honestly it's more like just a... stepping stone from here. Wasn't really set on going there but we didn't want to drive all the way to Vegas in one day."

"But isn't there a lot of film stuff there? Thought you'd be all over that."

She smirked, "Well, there's Hollywood, which I'll hopefully be at in a few years anyway, and there's the aqueduct where pretty much every film from Terminator to Drive has a scene... but I dunno, guess I'm just not feeling it." She leaned back, "I'd rather just spend it with you guys... just chilling really."

Grace nodded, "Fair enough, with all the driving we've been doing I guess we deserve a day to just take it easy."

"I second that." Eli stretched his fingers around the steering wheel, "Gets tiring doing the driving, happy to do it, but even happier not to."

"Well soon you won't have to." Emily laughed, "Only two hours till we reach LA."

"Two hours?" Grace groaned, "Fuuck. What are we going to do in the meantime?"

She shrugged, "Think up a game."

"I-Spy?"

"No."

"Truth or Dare?"

"Hell no! That would be a complete disaster!"

Grace threw her hands up in the air, "Well what do you suggest then? I'm coming up dry here!"

Emily pursed her lips, "How about cards?"

She shook her head, "Can't, they're in the back with everything else."

"Why wouldn't you keep them with you?"

"Why would I keep them with me?"

"You know," Emily shrugged like it was the most obvious thing in the world, "In case you needed them?"

She screwed her eyes up in utter confusion, "What possible scenario would I be in where I would need a fresh pack of cards on hand? I'm not fucking David Blaine, I'm not gonna Copperfield our way into a free hotel room!"

Emily put her hands up, "You wanted suggestions, I gave you suggestions."

"No, you didn't! You gave me one suggestion, and it was subpar! It was a..." She screwed the side of her mouth up to stop from laughing, "Sub-gestion."

"God!" Eli rolled his eyes, "Screw you both for making me listen to this!"

"You don't have to stay here Eli!"

"Oh wow, yeah, good suggestion. Just let me ninja roll my way out of this car..."

They giggled in the backseat, Emily looking and seeing Grace's face filled with mirth. Even though it had been hours, it was still hard to believe that everything really was working out, that the three of them were almost back to normal again. Though, given the truths that they'd found out about each other, and what Eli told her last night, she knew that tonight's talk was going to be tough on all of them. She just had to wait and hope that they were all willing to see it through, and be there for each other.

If she had of thought of this talk three days ago, she would have been petrified.

Now though, she could almost look forward to it. She learned something new about her friends, and for better or worse, there was no denying that they were all the closer for it. Hopefully they would feel the same way.

They pulled into LA as it was starting to get dark, and they'd heard enough horror stories about the city to know that they didn't want to be on the streets at night. Granted, a lot of those stories were probably exaggerated, but they couldn't fight the feeling they had anyway.

Eli pulled up in front of a liquor store, citing a need to get something to drink for all of them before the talk. The others couldn't help but agree. After purchasing a reasonably cheap bottle of whiskey, they made their way to what they could feel was a comparatively safer area of LA.

The car was parked and turned off, none of them making a move to leave. Eli turned around and looked at Emily, and it was a few seconds before she realized Grace was looking at her too.

"What? Why are you guys staring at me like that?"

They went back and forth, debating who should ask her, when Grace relented, "We were thinking... uh... do you want one bed? Or two again?"

"We just figured we should ask, cause like... if it would make you uncomfortable or anything like that..."

"No!" Feeling she was a bit too frantic with her answer, she paused, "I mean... this looks a lot nicer than the usual places we've stayed at huh? May as well save some money you know?"

Grace was unimpressed, "Em..."

"Alright fine, being close to you guys would be nice as well. Can I go now?"

Eli smiled, "Sure Em, just send us a message when we should come meet you."

She started to get out of the car, before turning and smirking at Grace, "You mind if I grab those cards? Might be able to do a magic trick and get them to give us the room for free."

"Fuck you!" She laughed, pushing Emily out with her foot, "Don't leave us waiting forever Em!"

"No way. Never gonna leave you waiting."

As soon as they stepped off the elevator nerves kicked in, the knowledge of what was waiting behind their room door heavy on their minds. They paused in front of the door, taking a second to breathe and look at each other.

"Alright, Eli looks like he ate something bad at dinner," She looked to Grace, "You look like you'd rather be anywhere but here, and I feel like I'm going to faint any second now." She clapped her hands, "I think we're ready, wouldn't you say?"

She turned the key and threw the door open, stepping in swiftly and sitting down on the bed. She put her head in her hands and took long, deep breaths, trying to will herself to calm down. After a few minutes of herself and her friends doing this, they felt confident enough to talk things through.

"So..." Grace shuffled, "Who should start?"

It was a few moments before Eli hesitantly held up his hand, "I think... I should go first."

They nodded, both sitting back to let him collect himself, "Alright... Grace, you'd say you're in love with Emily right? Not just attracted but... love, you know?"

She nodded, blushing furiously, "Yeah, I think that's pretty clear."

"And Emily, you love me and Grace, don't you?"

82

It felt much less scary to admit it this time, her reply almost instant, "Yes."

"Well..." Eli closed his eyes, breathing deeply. He looked at Grace, "Me too."

Grace smiled, "I know dude, we talked it through last night, it just feels good to get it out right?"

"No I..." He ran a hand over his face, willing his blush to go away, "I mean I..." She reached over and squeezed his hand, smiling gently to get him to speak. He exhaled roughly and looked into her eyes, "Grace I'm in love with you too."

The expression change was instantaneous, her eyes going wide and her jaw dropping open. It would have been hysterical if it weren't absolutely terrifying for Eli. "Grace? Grace come on, say something."

Emily shuffled over, putting a hand on Grace's shoulder and taking his other hand. Grace sat stock still, barely even breathing. "You... you're in love with *me* as well?"

He nodded, "Yeah, I have been for a long time now. I'm the same as Emily."

What came out of her mouth next was not what either of them expected, "You're the same as both of us."

"What?" Now it was their turn to pick their jaws up, "Grace... I know it's hard, believe me, but I need you to tell me exactly what you mean."

She sniffled, her eyes welling up even as a smile started to grace her lips, "You're in love with me and Em. She's in love with you and me. And I..." She wiped her eyes, a watery laugh coming from her lips, "I'm in love with both of you."

The room was silent for a few minutes afterwards, none of them daring to make a sound, lest the moment be completely ruined. After a justifiable period of stunned silence, Emily started to shake. While at first her friends were worried that she was crying, one look at the grin on her face and they could tell it wasn't the case. They were both incredibly confused, and moved over to put their hands on her back, "Em? I don't wanna sound stupid but... What the hell is so funny?"

She threw her head back and laughed, tears streaming down her cheeks, "We are so stupid! We could have had this worked out so long ago!" She wiped a tear from her eyes, breaking down into giggles once more, "Wh... How did we not know before now? How could we possibly have gone this long without knowing?"

"I guess... we just weren't looking for it." Eli snorted, small chuckles vibrating through his chest; "It does make us sound like idiots when you just lay it out like that though."

Grace grumbled to herself, "Could've spent so much time macking on each other already, had to leave it to the last minute..." She shook her head, "More importantly, uhh... what do we do now?"

"What do you mean?"

"What I mean is... well we all love each other right? So, what is this, some kind of... Jonestown, cult leader type shit we've got going on?"

"Actually, it'd be cult-y if we both loved Eli and didn't love each other, I think there has to be a leader for that sort of thing."

Eli held up his hand, "Wait, why am I the cult leader?" He shook his head, "No, wait, that doesn't matter. What does matter is... Well, what's wrong with all of us loving each other?"

"It's... weird, isn't it?" Grace screwed up her face, "Like... isn't more than two people cheating?"

"Normally it would be but I mean..." Emily shrugged, "Cheating kind of implies that someone doesn't know it'd be

happening, right? We're... very clear about what's happening."
She looked down, "Well I guess I did a cheating type thing before."

Eli shook his head, "You didn't start it with me, and Grace has already told you that you didn't start it with her." He smiled, "You gotta stop beating yourself up Em."

"I will eventually it's just... this is all so new to me."

Grace nodded, "To all of us really, I mean, what the hell do we even call this? I don't even know if there's a word for this!"

Eli shrugged, "Wouldn't it just be called dating?" His eyes went wide, "I mean, if you guys wanted to do that! I don't wanna put pressure on anyone or..."

Grace rolled her eyes, "Oh for Christ sake Eli, chill out. Going by the look Emily's face she's just as wiped by this as I am."

Emily smiled softly when she looked at him, reaching out to take his hand again, "We should probably tackle this again tomorrow, yeah?"

He smiled, shaking his head to himself. He got up and walked over to the bed, joining them under the covers, "I think that sounds great."

Grace took position on Emily's other side, "You know, one of these days I want to be in the middle..."

She laughed, "Maybe tomorrow." She snuggled in deeper between them, "For tonight, I'm taking advantage of this as much as I can."

Chapter Ten

"Have we ever told you how beautiful you look?"

Grace awoke with a start, looking around for the source of the voice. It shouldn't have come as a shock that she looked up to see Eli and Emily looking at her, but it did. So when she recoils backwards in surprise and off the bed entirely, she was too stunned to join in the laughter that followed.

"Holy shit Grace, are you ok?" Emily looked down at her, eyes wet from laughter and a hand extended.

Grace took it with a huff, sitting back up on the bed and crossing her arms, "That was mean you guys, seriously."

"You didn't answer our question though." Eli leaned over and smiled, "Have we ever told you?"

She looked down and blushed, very self-conscious all of a sudden, "I mean... not like this..."

Emily placed her hand on her knee, "Well, let's start now." She cleared her throat, "Grace, you are one of the most beautiful people I have ever seen in my life. We could reach the end of this road trip and see that meteor shower, and I would happily turn away from it, just for one chance to see another one of your smiles."

She was already a sputtering mess when Eli started up, "One of my favorite things in the world is seeing you happy. Did you know you almost literally brighten when you're in a good mood? Your cheeks light up, your eyes shine, it's like you just grabbed the sun and brought it down to the rest of us. You are truly beautiful Grace."

Emily nodded, "So wonderfully beautiful."

Her lip quivered, and before she could even attempt to hide away they wrapped her in their arms. She cried, her sounds muffled by their bodies, but these weren't from sorrow. It had been a long time since she had cried purely from experiencing something so beautiful, and she could already tell that there was going to be no forgetting the beauty in their words.

"Hey uh..." She started hesitantly after extracting herself from their arms, "I just... had a thought. Was wondering if you guys would be down for it."

"Probably, yeah." Emily smirked, "But just to be safe I'd like to hear it first."

Eli chuckled, but nodded as well.

She blew out a breath and pushed on, "So I know we're on the same page now with each other, but I was thinking... What if we get jealous?"

"I don't really see that happening..."

"I know! Believe me, I have good feelings here but... what about a test?"

Emily raised an eyebrow, "A... Test?"

She nodded, "Yeah. Eli kisses you first, and then I do. Only if it's ok with you though!"

"I... yeah, I'm fine with that." She turned, "Eli?"

"No problems here, believe me."

She chuckled, "Of course not. Wait..." She looked between him and Grace, "What about you and Eli? Shouldn't that be in the test as well?"

"I thought about that but... That might be a bit much for me right now. I'm still getting used to the idea of everything." She shrugged, "Sorry El."

He shook his head, "Oh trust me, I'm the exact same way. I want to, don't get me wrong but... yeah, too much too soon probably."

Emily breathed out, facing Eli, "Alright tiger, hit me with your best shot."

He moved in, "You're the worst."

Their lips connected, and this time there was no alcohol to muddy their senses, no guilt to push them away. There was only desire, and the burning need to make up for what they were only realizing was so much lost time. Grace watched in a daze, seeing their lips and tongues working in tandem, the way that she chased every kiss with a peck, the way he ran a hand along the back of her head almost reverently, as if she were a work of art. She felt a lot of things, amazement, happiness, a burning, feverish desire, but she noticed one thing that she wasn't feeling in the slightest.

Jealousy.

They jumped initially when they felt her hands on theirs, but soon were smiling into the kisses. When they pulled back they didn't just look into each other's eyes, they looked into hers.

"That... was beautiful. Now that I would gladly trade a meteor shower to see."

"Hardy har Gray." Eli pulled her in, trading places with her, "Your turn. Don't let me down now, I put my all into that you know."

The kiss that her and Emily shared was a much different affair to see, mainly because he was viewing it over Grace's extended middle finger. Whereas he poured himself into the kiss with a slow, careful touch, Grace dove in headfirst. Their kiss was all tongue and teeth, each of them sinking their teeth into the others' lower lip and tugging. The sounds that they made would be hard to forget, and indeed he had no intention of even attempting so. Though it was going to be very awkward when they looked back over at him. Grace ran her hand lightly over Emily's throat, her fingers closing lightly around it, not squeezing, but making it very clear that her hand was resting there.

How... interesting.

Finally, after what felt like an eternity of watching, they pulled back from each other breathless and flushed. They looked at the color of the others; face and giggled, foreheads leaning against each other as they breathed. He was praying for them not to look at him, and unfortunately his prayers were not heard.

"So did you enjoy..." Grace's cheeks lit up, Emily broke out in the widest grin he'd ever seen. Meanwhile he was praying for a rock to appear that he could hide under for the rest of his life.

"Clearly..." Emily snorted, trying not to outright lose it, "Clearly you enjoyed it..." She ran a hand over her mouth, attempting to wipe her smirk away, "But what about everything else? How do you feel?"

He smiled, still incredibly red, but happy that's all it was, "I feel good. No jealousy, no anger, no... nothing. I just..." He looked into both their eyes, "You were right Grace. It's beautiful."

"I'm half tempted to ask if you want to try it out, but let's not push our luck."

She nodded, "Smart, we gotta get to Vegas anyway. I haven't seen anything to like in LA so far, and I know for a fact that there are literally thousands of photo ops on the Strip."

"What are we waiting for then?" Emily pulled them both to their feet, smoothing out her shirt, "The sooner we get to the Strip, the sooner you can get famous!"

"So I hate to like, look a gift horse in the mouth and everything, but why are you suddenly deciding to drive now?" Eli looked over Emily's shoulder, trying to gauge the look on her face.

She smirked, "I figure this way we can still talk and everything, you know, the reason we became friends in the first place?"

"But like, couldn't you do that still if me or El was driving?" Grace raised an eyebrow, "Why would that change?"

"Because..." She looked in the rear-view mirror at them, "Now that we've worked things out, if I was back there with either one of you we wouldn't be doing any talking for the next five hours."

"Well I guess I would do the sa- *Five hours*?" Grace smacked her head against the back of the seat, "Why do I always forget how long it takes to go places?"

Eli chuckled, "Don't worry Grace, we can spend that next five hours talking. You know," He shot a look at Emily, "It's the reason we're friends."

"Are you going to take *everything* I ever say and throw it back at me?"

"Yes."

Grace cut in, "Actually, I was thinking about something." The others looked at her, "Well, what the fuck is everyone else going to say when they find out about this?" She waved her hands, "I mean, I don't really care what they say... but what do you think they'll say?"

"Man, I don't know." Eli looked to the ceiling, then started laughing, "Who would have seen this happening?"

Suddenly Emily couldn't help but remember her brother's words to her before they left. She groaned and let her head hit the dashboard, "Fuuuuuuck."

"Em? What's up?" She turned and looked at the two of them, faces full of concern.

She chuckled, "I think everyone knew actually."

"What?"

"My brother said that he thought that me and Grace had been girlfriends for the last three years. He also said that there was obviously something between the three of us."

"Oh..." Eli scratched the back of his neck, "That's pretty... perceptive of him."

"Yeah..." She worried, "Well... He also said that he wasn't the only one who thought so."

"Wait," Grace's eyes widened, "Who else knew?"

"I believe he insinuated that it's not exactly an uncommon way of thinking."

"Oh my god," Grace covered her face, "Just fucking shoot me now."

"People are going to be insufferable with the 'I told you so' crap." Eli shrugged, "Whatever, we still win."

Emily nodded, "Yes, yes we do."

The Strip was breathtaking, the lights as far as the eye could see, the crowds that never seemed to thin. It was pure and utter chaos, a complete assault on the senses, and they adored every minute of it.

"Over there! That sign looks fucked up, it's spelling the wrong thing!" Grace bounded through the streets, truly in her element. She shouldered her way past drunk, middle-aged men and retired, sun kissed old women, taking up residence on top of a table to get her perfect angle.

"You know, sometimes I forget just how much she loves this. Just like I forget how much you love film, and sometimes I forget my love of music."

Emily nodded, "We found the things in life that we can truly adore, the things we'd spend our life pursuing. Not everyone gets to experience that." She smiled to herself, linking their hands, "Not everyone gets to experience it more than once either."

He grinned, "Ok, over the last few days we've all said some pretty cheesy stuff." He pressed a kiss to her forehead, "That is by and large the cheesiest shit so far."

"You love it, don't deny."

"I didn't deny, did you hear me deny?"

"Kinda sounded like you were denying."

"Well I assure you, no denial here."

"Well..." Emily leaned forward and pressed her lips against his, relishing in the breathless gasp she got in return, "Good."

"Well well..." Grace threw herself between them, "I leave for two minutes and you two are already trying to eat each other." She tsked and shook her head, "What am I going to do with you two deplorable people?"

Emily shrugged, "Join in?"

She leaned in and captured Emily's lips with her own, "Goddamn right I am."

They were about to leave when they heard a throat clearing behind them. Grace turned, obviously ready for a confrontation if it went that way, but paused when she saw who was in front of her.

"Um, hello." A shorter woman, likely in her mid-30s, waved at them, an apologetic smile on her face, "Sorry to interrupt, really, but are you a photographer?"

Grace nodded, "Yeah, not professional or anything like that, but I love it."

The woman chuckled, "I could tell, you don't exactly jump on a table and kick over someone's chess set to capture a photo unless you truly care." She held out her hand, "Sandra."

Grace returned the handshake, "Grace, what do you need Sandra?"

"Well, I was wondering if I could take a quick look at your photographs." She looked over to Emily and Eli, "Assuming you don't have to be somewhere in a hurry."

They shook their heads, "If Grace is fine with it, take all the time you need."

"Brilliant!" She inclined her head at an empty bench, "Shall we?"

"Yeah, sure." Grace was still immensely confused by the exchange, but was more than willing to share her work with someone who was interested.

She sat next to Sandra, already going through her camera's memory to find her favorite shots. As they passed each one, Sandra gave both praise and criticism on each on, though she found it worth noting that there was far more praise. After the twentieth photo Grace finally needed to know exactly why she was doing this.

"Uh, Sandra?" The woman looked up at her, eyebrow raised, "I'm glad to be doing this, don't get me wrong but... Why are you so interested?"

"Oh, did I not tell you?" Sandra shook her head, "I'm always forgetting to do that. I run a gallery in Portland, I think your work would fit in well there."

Grace's jaw dropped, as did Emily and Eli's when they overheard, "I... I'm sorry, you run *what*?"

"A gallery?" She smiled, "What's so strange about that?"

"I... you're interested in me? I'm not a professional, I'm just an amateur!"

"Everyone's an amateur until they become a professional, how do you think that happens?"

Grace rubbed her neck, "This is insane, you just come out of nowhere and tell me you think my work would fit in..."

"Oh, it's not think anymore, I know it'll fit in." She pointed at the latest photo, "See this? Your composition is perfect, the angles are pleasing to the eye, but you pack so much meaning into a simple picture of a broken sign. A statement of the decay of the old ways of society, while newness thrives around it." She smiled, "Trust me, you could be a professional easily, you just need to take the first step."

Grace looked close to crying, so she relented and sat back.

"Now, I know this is a lot to take in, trust me I know." She scribbled on a piece of paper, "This is my contact number and email address. You get in touch with me whenever you are ready to take that first step, it could be ten minutes from now, it could be a year from now. Whenever you are ready."

She nodded mutely. Sandra stood and squeezed her shoulder, looking at the other two, "It was lovely to meet you all."

She was long gone by the time the three of them returned to their senses, and even then they couldn't properly say what they were thinking. Emily walked forward slowly, her mouth uselessly trying to form words. "I... you... she..." She grabbed Grace's shoulders, leaning in and looking her square in the eye, "You're a fucking star."

Grace surged forward, grabbing handfuls of Emily's hair and pulling their lips deeper together. It must have been quite the scene, because Eli cleared his throat,

"Guys? Not that I'm not thrilled to see this... but maybe we'd better continue at the hotel, yeah?"

Chapter Eleven

They woke up the next morning to a problem. A very, very serious problem.

"Guys?" Emily looked at her phone in fear, her hand shaking, "If we don't get some more money soon, we're not gonna be able to get back to Seattle."

"Are you serious?" Eli looked over her shoulder, his eyes going wide in sudden dread, "Oh. Oh *fuck*."

Grace took to pacing, not wanting to see the exact number herself, "Shit. Shit! What are we going to do?"

"We need to get money, fast! Or we're not going to be able to have much choice in what we do." Eli shook his head, "I don't want to have to be a hooker, not yet! I've still got so many things I want to do!"

"Calm down! No one's becoming a hooker!" Emily pinched the bridge of her nose, "We just need to sit down and think. How do we get money?"

Grace sat down and raised her hand, "Um... First of all... we're in Vegas? Just saying."

Eli shook his head, "Come on Gray, how many people come here every day thinking that's gonna work? The city survives on idiots like that!"

"Well someone has to win once in a while! Why can't it be us?"

"Probably because we need the money, it's never the poor people who win big here."

"Look just... trust me here guys." Grace laid her hands on the table, looking at each of them earnestly, "Let me just try the slot machines, no more than ten dollars."

"I jus-" Emily squeezed her eyes closed, "Fine, ten dollars. No more than that, we really can't spare it."

"Trust me." Grace grinned, "It'll be worth it."

They stepped onto the floor, the sound of chips and voices thunderous in the enclosed space. Even after seeing the Strip, they were astonished at the amount of people seated indoors.

"Holy crap. There's gotta be like... a thousand people in here."

"Well, let's pick a machine and get started," Eli nudged Grace forward, "I'm curious to see if this'll work or not."

She looked through the aisles, looking each machine up and down before moving on. After the twelfth aisle, Emily pulled her aside, "Gray? What are you doing?"

"I'm looking for one that takes one dollar per pull, most amount of chances you know? Only need a few hundred dollars anyway, don't need to get risky."

"This is already risky, but I get it."

They moved on, passing row after row, before finally they found the one they were looking for. Grace took her seat in front of one, noting that there wasn't anyone else in the row, "The other reason I wanted one like this, is because no one uses them. Everyone goes for the big dollar machines, hoping to win big and cash in a million. You're much more likely to win on one of these?"

"Why?" Eli tilted his head, "Because less people play them?"

"Duh." She scoffed, "These things are rigged as hell, no way are you ever gonna win the million. But one of these, that no one cares about and the top prize is ten thousand?" She smirked, "Damn right you'll win something!"

Her first pull was a dud. So was the second, and third. Every single one up to eight in fact. She leaned over the slot machine, groaning to herself, "My plan is foolproof, this can't be happening."

Emily shook her head, "Look, you've got two more pulls. Just take them and let's get out of here."

She straightened up, "Alright, here goes nothing." She pulled the lever, watching the number speed by. Each one stopping only made her heart beat faster, and the ding of the alarm almost stopped it completely. Chips spilled out the bottom, her two companions frantically picking them up.

"Fuck me Gray! You won like, a hundred dollars!" Eli looked at her in complete joy.

She furrowed her brow, "I did?" She looked down and grinned, "I did!"

They drew her in for a hug, squeezing her close, "I am never doubting you again Gray, never again." Emily flicked her head at the exit, "Let's get outta here yeah?"

"Sure thing..." She made to walk off, then remembered, "Oh wait! I have one more go!" She pulled the lever, the alarm going off once more soon after.

Eli's shout of glee was audible through the whole casino, "Another hundred Gray I *fucking love you*!"

"So two hundred dollars, that'll get us to... Eugene." Emily shook her head, "That's good, it really is, but we just need a bit more."

"But how?" Grace rested her head in her hands; "I think I used up the last of my luck on those slot machines, I think I'm tapped out."

Eli paced back and forth across the carpet, hand on his chin as he thought. Idea after idea flashed through his head, before he finally remembered their ace in the hole. He turned to them with a triumphant smile, "I got it!"

"This must be really good if it's got you this excited." Emily leaned forward, "Spill the beans."

He pointed at her, "You hustle pool!"

She closed her eyes, taking a deep breath, "That's it? That's your master plan?"

"No, I think he might be onto something..." Grace crossed her hands in front of her face, "You always kick our asses when we play."

"No offense, but that's because you guys suck."

"Alright look that's... true, but that doesn't mean that you aren't great!" Eli walked over and sat next to her, leaning on her shoulder, "Just try it, come on. Please?"

She rolled her eyes and smiled, "Dirty trick..."

The three sat themselves next to the window, they wanted to see exactly who would be arriving after all. The bar was a little on the outskirts of Vegas, still semi decent but with just enough lower quality aspects to be wary of. Thankfully for the most part the current crowd was civil, but who knew if that would hold up?

A quick practice run on the table annoyingly confirmed exactly what Emily suspected. She was good. Very good. God have mercy on the poor idiot she'd choose as her mark.

"Oh, this one pulling up, how about him?" Eli pointed out the window at the newest arrival. "Driving a brand new 4x4, stepping out with hair gelled back with at least two tubs of product, bellowing at his frat boy friends with one of the most unappealing laughs in recent memory?"

"Yep." Emily smirked, "That's the guy."

They waited until he got three drinks deep, and in that time any guilt they might have felt disappeared. He was loud, rude, dismissive to the barmaid... yep, he was the perfect target. By the time Eli approached him to suggest a game the owners looked close to kicking him out themselves.

"What's up my man?" Eli gave his most winning smile, "You play pool?"

The man turned to him, red cheeked and already swaying, "I wha- yeah, yeah I play pool."

He chuckled, this was too easy, "Well how about a game then? Fifty bucks says you can't beat me."

"Fifty bucks, fuck, you're on." He got up and almost toppled to the ground, before gathering himself and walking to the table. The owners shook their heads with a smile, they knew exactly what Eli was playing at. He gave a wink and turned back.

The first game went perfectly, Eli lost completely. To his private embarrassment, he wasn't faking being that bad. The drunk was whooping and hollering to his friends when Emily stepped up, "Hey big boy!" He turned at her voice, "Bet you can't beat *me* this time."

"Oh yeah?" He slurred, damn near licking his lips, "What do I get if I beat you?"

Emily's lip curled in disgust, "How about two hundred dollars? That good enough?"

He laughed, "Is that good enough?" He pulled out his wallet, showing it overstuffed with bills, "Honey I've got money comin' out my ass! You're on!"

She turned to grab the stick off Eli, smirking to herself. She leaned in close, her lips brushing Eli's ear, "I am going to *humiliate* this little man."

She walked away, leaving a jaw-dropped Eli behind her. "I don't think I've ever been this aroused in my life."

Grace snorted into her beer, "Great, I just found one of your kinks."

"So you want to go first darling?" The frat boy sneered, "Or do you like to mop up?"

"Why don't you go first Pillsbury? We'll see if you're disappointing right off the bat."

He growled and leaned forward, sweat already beading off his forehead. He skimmed the side of the cue ball, sending it careening into the side of the triangle. They scattered, but not a single one was sunk.

Emily chuckled, "How predictable." She leaned forward, "Watch how someone competent does it."

She was efficient, precise, each shot hitting its mark. By the time it was his turn again over half her balls had already been sunk. He looked at the table, sweat falling down his face from drunkenness and clear nervousness. He gulped, looking desperately for a shot to take.

Emily could see dozens of shots he could take, at least ten of which complete amateurs would be able to make with ease. But she had evidently rattled him very hard, his hands shaking so much that his shot only connected with one of hers, sending it into the pocket. She clapped, "Aw, thanks buddy. I could use a helping hand."

He was turning purple with anger, but kept it under control for the moment. The instant she sunk her last ball however, he exploded.

"Fuck you! That was bullshit! This shit was fucking rigged you bitch!" He was almost foaming at the mouth, his teeth bared. Emily wasn't backing down, and she narrowed her eyes in warning.

"I'd be real fucking careful about what you say next fratfuck. Now give me my money."

"Bullshit bet, you don't get *shit*!" She tightened her grip on the stick, Grace stepped forward and put her hand on her shoulder.

"Hey, Em, come on don't worry. Let's just calm down alright?"

He sneered at Grace, his eyes raking up and down her body, "Yeah sure, listen to your little pet there!"

Emily bared her teeth, fists clenching, "*What* did you just say?"

"Like I'm going to pussy out from some stupid bitch and her cunt fri-"

He didn't have time to finish his insult before Emily's fist connected with his jaw. He fell backwards and slumped down against the table, out cold and down at least one tooth. His three other friends looked on stunned for a second, before surging forwards themselves. The three companions for their part didn't hesitate at all, already picking which one they wanted and diving towards them.

Though they were drunk, the frat boys were far from the pushover that their leader was. Though Emily and Grace got in some good hits that left their opponents reeling, the exact same happened to them. Eli at least fared a bit better, tossing his frat boy right over the pool table.

The owners and other customers were no fan of fights happening on the premises, but they were even less enthused by the antics of drunken frat boys who through the whole night had shown nothing but disrespect. Thus, when two larger members of the crowd walked over to stop the fight, they were very clearly focused on helping the trio of friends. Things went awry however when Grace spat blood in her opponent's eye, his wild punch missing her completely and knocking one of the men to the ground.

The whole room seemed to stop, everyone absorbing exactly what had happened. Then in a flash, the crowd descended on them.

In between the shouting, the punching and even the biting, the three of them managed to crawl out of the crowd, keeping their heads down until they reached the outside. Eli and Emily began running to the car, while Grace suddenly stopped. Eli turned around and threw his hands out, "Grace what the fuck! Let's go!"

"One second!" She picked up a nearby bottle and smashed it along the ground, taking the broken glass and shoving it into the frat boy's tires. She started giggling, running off to join the others, "Take that you dumb assholes!"

The three of them sped off, Eli gripping the steering wheel tightly until they were well out of sight of the bar. They pulled up outside their hotel and just sat there, trying to absorb exactly what had just happened. Grace was the first to break, her body shaking with suppressed laughter, tiny giggles forcing their way out, "You... you fucked that guy up! *One shot*, bam!"

Eli smiled, "Fuck yea, remind me never to get in a fight with you Em!"

"What about you El?" She leaned forward and poked his shoulder, "Tossed that guy clean over the table like he was nothing!"

"To be fair, he *was* nothing." He grinned, "But thanks anyway, my ego could always use the boost."

Grace pouted, "It was fun, but still, we went there to get money. Now what? Now we're fucked."

Once again, the car was silent, none of them making a sound. They turned to Emily when they heard a giggle, seeing her face bright red and her lips stretched in delight, "I wouldn't say that exactly..." She held her hand up, a fat wallet clutched between her fingers.

Eli's eyes widened, "Is that..."

She nodded, "Dumbass left it on the table the whole time, I just grabbed it on the way out."

"How much is in there?" Grace looked at the bills sticking out, none below a twenty.

Emily smirked, "A lot."

Grace nodded, suddenly focused, "We need to get up to the room. Right now."

As soon as they were through the door they were all over each other, the three of them collapsing to the bed in a tangle as they tried to get to each other. Emily sat back, seeing Grace and Eli tentatively eyeing each other, pushing forward. Their lips met and she could swear she saw the sparks fly, the two of them adapting remarkably quickly.

Before she knew it they dragged her into their pile, her lips clumsily joining theirs in an exchange that none involved knew how to work. Their noses kept bumping, accidental pinches on their lips left them wincing momentarily, but none of them would describe the moment as anything less than perfect. In that moment they knew that everything was real. The feelings of closeness, of warmth, of sheer love were so intense that they would weep if they weren't otherwise occupied. And that's how they stayed for hours, passing back and forth between each other until they collapsed in an exhausted heap, their arms wrapped securely around one another.

Chapter Twelve

"God, I can't believe the moment is almost here." Eli looked up at the afternoon sky, the Grand Canyon stretching out in front of him. He took a breath of the fresh air, holding it and letting it out slowly.

Grace walked up and took his arm, "I know... Can you believe how much has changed in like... Nine days?"

"Trust me, I have a hard time believing it as well." Emily laughed from behind them, putting the finishing touches on their tent. She stepped back, clapping her hands together once she was certain it wouldn't blow away unexpectedly. "If you'd told me we'd be doing this... Shit, you told me I was in love with you guys and I would've laughed my ass off."

"Oh no," Grace looked down, smirking to herself, "That would've been a tragedy."

Emily drew her hand back and brought it forward with a smack, Grace squeaking as she lifted herself upwards in surprise. She almost whimpered when Emily leaned into her ear, "Keep talking like that, and you might get to see it later."

Grace gulped, a shaky smile coming over her face, "C-can't wait."

"But right now, I think it's time we cracked some of these bottles open." She grinned as she popped a cap off, "Thank god for frat boys."

Eli shook his head, picking up his own bottle, "Still can't believe that worked out, guess karma was on our side."

"Well, I'm not complaining." She clinked her bottle against his, reaching down and passing Grace her own, "Come on Grace, drink up."

"Don't have to tell me twice." She leaned back in one of the lawn chairs that had been set up, "So, this is it huh? What we came here to see?" She smiled softly, "Gotta admit, I'm gonna be sad when it's over."

Emily nodded, "I thought I would be too, but..." She looked at the both of them, "We got something so much more out of it."

"True." Eli nodded, "Very true." He chuckled, "Man, your brother is gonna have a field day with this."

"God, don't remind me." She threw her head back and groaned, "Makes me almost not want to go home."

"Yeah you say that now, but just think about how soft it'd be. How warm, the covers would be thick and just wrap around you..." Grace trailed off, Emily raised an eyebrow.

"Grace... Do you want to have sex with my *bed*?"

She laughed, "No you weirdo! I'm just kinda getting tired of hotel beds, no matter how clean. I just want to go home and sleep for like, a year."

"That sounds so good..." Eli chuckled, "I tell you, after this trip I'm not getting into another car for at least a month, I've had enough of driving to last me a freaking lifetime."

"Well you can relax for now El. After tonight, there's no real deadline to get anywhere, we can sleep in for as long as we want. No one can stop us." She closed her eyes and readied for a quick nap, "No one."

"Em? Hey, Em?" She woke to someone jostling her shoulder. Shaking away and sitting up slowly she saw that Grace was the one doing it. "Hey sleepy head, how you doing?" She smiled at Emily, slowly rubbing her arm as she woke up.

Emily ran a hand over her eyes, "W-What time is it?"

"About eight, it's supposed to be starting really soon." She pulled her to her feet, "Come on, get a move on. Don't wanna miss the show, do we?"

They walked over to where Eli had planted himself, hands on hips and staring directly upwards. They were all silent as the time approached, and just as they were tempted to look away, it happened. A flash, a streak of light, so sudden they could have imagined it.

Then another, and another.

The sky lit up above them, dozens of streaks of light falling across the night as they passed by. Emily wasn't sure when it happened, but she noticed she was crying. Looking to the side, she saw that they were as well.

She reached out, taking each of their hands in her own. They closed their eyes, letting the moment take over. "This is it, this is a turning point for all of us. Being here, with you, seeing something like this..." She smiled, "I don't think I can ever forget it. If either of you are having second thoughts, I won't hold it against you. But now is the time to say it."

They squeezed her hands back, looking at her with pure conviction, "No, no second thoughts. No regrets." Grace nodded, "We love you Em. We *always* will."

She sniffled, letting a tear flow freely as she pulled them along, "Then come on. I want... I want to share everything with you."

Their eyes widened, they knew what she meant by that. But neither of them were nervous, or scared. They just wanted to make sure it was done right.

They fell on to the floor of the tent, shuffling up onto the sleeping bags to get comfortable. They laughed and giggled when their backs touched the cold material, drawing each other closer to warm up.

"Em... Are you sure you want to do this?" Eli pulled back, looking her in the eye, "We can wait as long as you need, don't worry."

She grabbed him by the collar and pulled him down, silencing him with her lips. The tent was silent save for the sound of their mingled breathing, Emily running a soothing hand along Grace's leg. She pulled back, looking at the both of them, "I want this. I'm sure of it, are you?"

They both smiled, "If you are, we are."

She sat up, her hands grabbing hold of the hem of her shirt. She took a deep breath, letting it out as she lifted. Her friends sat transfixed, the sight in front of them one of the most incredible things they'd seen in their life. Emily blushed, the color reaching past her face all the way down to her now bare chest. She chuckled nervously, "God you guys, stop staring, it's embarrassing."

Grace giggled, "Sorry, sorry." She reached forward, cupping one of her breasts, "Is... is this ok?"

Her reply was breathless, "Yes..." She beckoned to Eli, "Please... you too."

He obliged, squeezing and stroking along her globe, "Jesus Christ Emily, you're so fucking beautiful."

She moaned, leaning back on the bags. They followed, not long after nodding to each other. They attached their mouths to her breasts, the wail she made in response a memory they would cherish. She ran her hands through their hair, tugging and pushing in equal measure. Finally, she pulled them both up, "Please, I need to see you."

They smiled, more than happy to do as she asked. With very little apprehension they stripped down, their clothing joining

Emily's in the corner to be forgotten until the morning. The three of them sat still, taking a moment to absorb each other's forms. Any awkwardness was quickly forgotten, replaced by white-hot flames of desire. Eli smirked at Emily, "You look like you're getting desperate."

She rolled her eyes, "I need one of you, it honestly doesn't matter to me which one."

He looked at Grace, shrugging, "Do you... Do you want to go first?"

She raised her eyebrow, "Are you sure?"

"Yeah, don't worry about it. I've... gotta get ready anyway." He smiled, "Besides, this trip was for you anyway, did you forget that?"

"You dorks." She crawled over to Emily, cupping her head in her hands. She slowly pressed their lips together, her tongue pushing through her lips and tasting. She dragged her hand lower, brushing over a nipple and leaving Emily shivering. When she reached her waistband they both froze, looking into each other's eyes. "Last chance." When Emily nodded she pressed a quick kiss to her nose, before slipping her hand under. As soon as her fingers made contact Emily arched her back, what she didn't know she wanted for so long finally happening.

Grace jumped as she felt more fingers brush against her, looking back and seeing Eli leaning over, "El? What are you doing?"

He grunted as he undid the button on Emily's pants and started to pull them down, "It's not fair if you're the only one who gets to watch."

She ran her finger up and down, before finally, mercifully pushing two in. She pushed in and Emily tensed, she crooked her fingers and Emily almost wept. She grabbed onto Grace's shoulders, anchoring her body, before thrusting herself back and forth.

Looking onward, Eli wasn't sure what to do with himself other than stare. The image of Emily frantically, almost feverishly riding Grace's hand while she braced her, locking their lips together passionately... it was an image that would imprint itself on his very retinas.

Grace could tell she was starting to get close, so she offered a push in the right direction. She extended her thumb, flicking it over the sensitive bundle of nerves above her core. Emily ceased to even make words, reduced to primal grunts and chokes. It was barely a minute later before her eyes rolled back in her head and she trembled around Grace's fingers. She pumped a few more times, helping her ride out the aftershocks, before slowly withdrawing her fingers, the feeling making Emily shudder.

"Hey Em... You feel ok?" She kissed her forehead, a worried smile on her face.

Emily grinned, pulling her down again, "More than ok. But what about Eli?" She looked over her shoulder, "He looks like he's in pain over there."

"I'm good!" He grit his teeth, "Take as long as you need to calm down, I'll be fine!"

"I think we've all done enough waiting, don't you?" She reached out for him, "Now I'm telling you, get over here. I'll be fine."

He smiled devilishly, "Yes ma'am." Shuffling over, he pressed a kiss to her chest before he lined himself up with her entrance. One final time, he looked up at her, "Are you going to be ok?"

"Alright I'll admit that you're a bit bigger than I thought you'd be but..."

He rolled his eyes, "That's not what I meant, ass, and you know it."

"Trust me Eli, if I wasn't ready I'd tell you." She wiggled her hips impatiently, "Now hurry up and fuck me!"

He pressed himself against her, resistance minimal before he began to slowly sink in. Her mouth opened in a silent moan as her body took more and more of him, his length disappearing bit by bit within her. Once he was fully sheathed they let out the breaths that they'd both been holding, laughing together.

"So, guess we've gone and done it now."

"Yeah," She nodded, grinning, "Guess we have." She flicked her head, "You can start moving you know."

He began to thrust his hips, slowly and shallowly at first, but as he felt her relax more he upped his pace. She ran a hand up and down his stomach, the fleeting touches and delicate pinches feeling like electricity against his bare skin.

"Holy crap." Grace leaned in, watching intently where they were connected, their grunts and other obscene sounds pure music to her ears. He picked up the pace when he remembered that they had an audience, and he intended to give them a show. Emily wasn't complaining, having to clutch onto one of the bags behind her to stop from being thrown around the tent from the force of his thrusts, certain that the sound of their coupling must be audible down in the valley.

Grace smirked as an idea came to her head, "You guys might kill me for doing this... but whatever." Before they could ask what she was doing she leaned into Eli's stomach, extending her tongue and laving it across his skin. He groaned at the contact, only dimly feeling her descending. When he realized what she was doing, he looked down with wide eyes, watching as she dragged her tongue along his length and to where their bodies were meeting. She lavished attention on Emily's core, the combination of the feeling and the sight too much for both of them to take. He thrust twice more before slamming himself deep, groaning harshly, his vision going white. Emily tightened around him a second later, her orgasm hitting her hard and fast. They collapsed in a boneless heap, Grace giggling to herself as she wiped her mouth.

"You... you *cheeky fucker*." Eli laughed as he looked up at her, still smiling like the Cheshire Cat.

"I got bored of watching, don't know how you stuck it out so long." She leaned down, dragging him in for a deep kiss; "You got any of that for me?"

He gasped as she tugged on his lip, "Miraculously, yeah, I do."

"Good." She placed a hand on his chest, "Don't get up, you're good like that."

He leaned his head back and let her get into position, placing his hands on her hips to feel the shift of her powerful muscles underneath the skin. She lowered herself all at once, caution being thrown to the wind in her quest for satisfaction. "Yep," She gasped, "We *really* should have figured this out sooner, we could have done this so much earlier!"

Eli couldn't answer, too distracted by the mesmerizing movements her body made as it moved up and down upon him. It only got worse when Emily finally recovered, slinking up behind Grace and taking hold of her chest. Dragging her head back she dug her tongue into Grace's mouth, the sight in front of him truly something worthy to be made into a painting. Emily took one hand off Grace's chest, tracing it down her stomach and to directly to her core. She smirked into her mouth, "Time for a little payback."

With one hand still furiously palming her breasts, she flicked her other fingers over Grace's clit. She was edging, desperate to get just enough to tip over the edge. When Emily not only pinched her nipple, but pulled, she fell over the edge screaming.

She shuddered around Eli, the last of his release forcing its way out before they all collapsed together, desperate to not have to make another move except to drag the cover over themselves. It was an eternity before their minds were free enough to think, and true to form it was Grace who spoke first.

"I'm gonna take that opportunity in Portland."

They smiled, eyes filled with warmth, "We thought you would, it's everything you want after all."

"I still want to travel and everything but... yeah, this is something I've wanted my whole life, and it almost literally fell into my lap."

Emily raised an eyebrow, "So, what are you going to do?"

She thought for a second before nodding, "Pretty soon I'll move to Portland, rent a place for a few weeks, maybe a month or two. I'll get things sorted out with the gallery, see if I can work from off site, submit my stuff that way."

"And then?"

She smiled, "And then I'm going to follow you guys. I'm going to be in and out, you know, but... if you guys'll have me I... I'd love to be with you. I think that's what I want more than anything."

They squeezed her as tight as they could, heads resting on her shoulders as they covered her, "We want nothing more in the world than to be with you. No matter how long it takes, how often you leave, we want to be with you. Without you, there's no us, not really." Emily smiled at the two of them, "This was meant to be, I just never knew it until recently. I couldn't imagine my life without you two."

"Me neither." Eli pressed a kiss to both of their cheeks, Grace relaxed her body and closed her eyes.

"This is how our lives are meant to be."

"Do you know what this feeling is? This one, right here?"

Emily curled around them and closed her eyes.

"It feels like home."